Silence greeted Bolan as he cracked open the door

Throwing it wide, he sprinted toward a wooden fence and stared over the top at a pair of bodies sprawled in an alley. Policemen judging by their uniforms. Glancing up, he spotted a lone figure fleeing toward the mouth of the alley.

The man looked back once and kept going.

In that brief moment the figure's stocky silhouette gave Bolan a clue to the killer's identity. Only one member of the Black Hand had that build — Orhan Mithat.

The Executioner slowed as he neared the street and cautiously peered around the corner. Mithat was a block away, just entering a park.

As sirens blared in the distance, Bolan realized the peril of pursuing a terrorist in Turkey. Any Turkish cop, unaware of the situation, might shoot him down, mistaking him for the murderer.

The warrior was almost to the park when he detected movement in his peripheral vision. Even as his mind registered the motion, a submachine gun opened fire.

MACK BOLAN®

The Executioner

DON PENDLETON'S
THE **EXECUTIONER**®
FEATURING **MACK BOLAN**®

BLACK HAND

A GOLD EAGLE BOOK FROM
WORLDWIDE.

TORONTO • NEW YORK • LONDON
AMSTERDAM • PARIS • SYDNEY • HAMBURG
STOCKHOLM • ATHENS • TOKYO • MILAN
MADRID • WARSAW • BUDAPEST • AUCKLAND

First edition October 1993

ISBN 0-373-61178-1

Special thanks and acknowledgment to
David Robbins for his contribution to this work.

BLACK HAND

A man without freedom is conceivable only as a man bereft of life.

—Leo Tolstoy
War and Peace

I'm not a man who takes the right to freedom lightly. Whether at home or abroad, when those who want to strip us of that right try to do so, I intend to be there to stop them.

—Mack Bolan

THE
MACK BOLAN®
LEGEND

Nothing less than a war could have fashioned the destiny of the man called Mack Bolan. Bolan earned the Executioner title in the jungle hell of Vietnam.

But this soldier also wore another name—Sergeant Mercy. He was so tagged because of the compassion he showed to wounded comrades-in-arms and Vietnamese civilians.

Mack Bolan's second tour of duty ended prematurely when he was given emergency leave to return home and bury his family, victims of the Mob. Then he declared a one-man war against the Mafia.

He confronted the Families head-on from coast to coast, and soon a hope of victory began to appear. But Bolan had broken society's every rule. That same society started gunning for this elusive warrior—to no avail.

So Bolan was offered amnesty to work within the system against terrorism. This time, as an employee of Uncle Sam, Bolan became Colonel John Phoenix. With a command center at Stony Man Farm in Virginia, he and his new allies—Able Team and Phoenix Force—waged relentless war on a new adversary: the KGB.

But when his one true love, April Rose, died at the hands of the Soviet terror machine, Bolan severed all ties with Establishment authority.

Now, after a lengthy lone-wolf struggle and much soul-searching, the Executioner has agreed to enter an "arm's-length" alliance with his government once more, reserving the right to pursue personal missions in his Everlasting War.

PROLOGUE

Ankara, Turkey

At ten minutes past noon the green van turned onto tree-lined Ataturk Bulvari, more commonly known as Embassy Row, and cruised westward at the speed limit. It passed the Italian and Russian Embassies, approaching the American compound.

The Turks inside both had dark hair, a dark mustache and brown eyes. The driver was a tall man, with a nasty scar that ran from the outer corner of his left eye to the corner of his mouth. His passenger had a stocky build and wore a devious grin, as if he were smiling at a joke only he knew. Both wore black.

The two Marine guards standing just inside the wrought-iron embassy gate were being kept busy, opening and closing the gate for staffers departing for lunch. Only the senior Marine, a corporal, happened to glance up and spy the van as he started to pull the portal open for a man about to leave. Since he'd seen many such delivery vans during his tour as a guard, the corporal thought nothing of it.

The van accelerated suddenly and jinked toward the embassy. For a moment the stocky Turk disappeared.

When he popped up again he held an Uzi. The driver raised a pistol.

The corporal frantically tried to close the gate, but with a harsh crash the vehicle struck the barrier dead center, battering it wide open, throwing the Marines off balance. Both Turks leaned out their windows and opened fire, slaying the corporal and the second Marine on the spot. An embassy staffer in a station wagon was also brutally gunned down.

Moments later the tall Turk brought the van to a screeching stop at the base of the embassy steps and both men leaped out, as did three others from the back, two women and a man armed with Uzis, all wearing black. One of the women stayed with the vehicle as the rest pounded up the steps and dashed inside.

A receptionist and a young Marine running down a winding stairway were taken out with a blistering hail of lead.

Wasting no time, the four Turks started up the stairs. They almost reached the next landing when another Marine appeared, his pistol extended. A single shot caught the scarred Turk in the right shoulder, spinning him. The other three returned fire, stitching the Marine from crotch to throat.

Grimacing, the injured man clutched his shoulder and led his companions onward. A polished mahogany door barred their path, but not for long. They crashed through into a plush office where a blond secretary was talking excitedly on the phone. Her eyes widened in terror a split second before a hole blossomed in her forehead.

The savage quartet raced to a door situated beyond her desk, the tall Turk grinning triumphantly. The third man smashed it open with a swift kick. Within lay a spacious, ornate, unoccupied chamber, a huge oak desk at the very center.

His grin changing to furious disappointment, the tall Turk stalked into the room, still clutching his shoulder, and glared at the empty furniture.

"He's not here, Muzo," the stocky man said. "Let's go."

The man called Muzo pounded his fist on top of the desk. "The gardener sold us the wrong schedule!"

"Maybe the ambassador changed it at the last minute," the woman suggested, her brown eyes darting nervously about.

But Muzo appeared not to hear. Scowling, he angrily kicked over a chair. "I'll rip Vahdettin's face off!"

"You can take care of him later," the stocky Turk stated. "We have to leave before the rest of the Marines show up."

Muzo nodded reluctantly and made for the doorway. "You're right, Orhan. Let's go."

They raced down the stairs, charging across the lobby just as a pair of embassy personnel emerged from a door along the right-hand wall. The female terrorist promptly spun and cut them down.

"Nice shooting, Yeni," Orhan observed.

"Move it!" Muzo barked, reaching the entrance first. He held the door for the others, then bounded down the steps to the van.

Inside the embassy an alarm finally sounded, blaring stridently. From the distance came the wail of police sirens.

"Get in the van," Muzo bellowed, and glanced at the woman who had watched the vehicle. "The ambassador wasn't there, Nur."

Her short hair bobbing as she swung toward the rear door, Nur looked at him, her hawkish features reflecting her annoyance. "The damn gardener betrayed us."

"My thoughts exactly." Muzo ran around the front to climb behind the wheel as his companions piled inside. He shifted into drive, stepped on the gas, executed a tight U-turn and they were gone.

1

Mack Bolan, a.k.a. the Executioner, ignored a mosquito that buzzed his face and concentrated on the placid cove north of his position. Soon, he told himself. According to the informant who provided the intel to the Turkish authorities, the gunrunners planned to bring in their cargo at midnight. Ten minutes remained.

From where he lay on a low, grassy knoll, he could just distinguish the twin points of land jutting into the Black Sea on either side of the cove. His blue eyes narrowed as he scanned the glassy surface and listened for the telltale growl of a speedboat engine.

Nothing yet.

The warrior propped his elbows on the ground, raised his M-16 to his shoulders and pressed his right eye to the hyperminiscope night sight mounted on the rifle. Adjusting the magnification factor to X6, he focused on the three men standing twenty-five yards away on the narrow strip of shore.

They were Turks, and a hefty man on the right cradled an SB-30 light machine gun, minus the customary bipod, in his brawny hands. The SB-30 was in widespread use in Iran, Turkey's southeastern neighbor, and it was easy to imagine a few stolen crates making their way secretly into the country.

In the center stood a thin man, a crafty devil who had been engaged in smuggling for more than three decades and had earned the nickname of the Fox because he always stayed one step ahead of the law. His hands were empty but there was a suspicious bulge under his blue jacket, on his right hip.

On the left was another hardman, one of the Fox's bodyguards who had an M-26 submachine gun tucked under his left elbow. Not the stoic type, he kept fidgeting from foot to foot and glancing in all directions.

Bolan let his finger lightly touch the trigger. At such short range they would be candy. He wondered if the sound of the shots would carry to Akcakoca, the small town less than a mile to the east. If so, and even if someone came to investigate, Arpinar and his boys would take care of the curious.

Thinking of Mehmet Arpinar brought to mind a whole string of memories. Two days earlier Bolan had heard about the attack on the U.S. Embassy in Ankara. That same evening he'd been summoned to a meet with Hal Brognola and given a personal request from the President.

Brognola, the troubleshooting Fed who served as director of the Sensitive Operations Group for the United States Department of Justice, had been his usual blunt self. "Striker," he'd declared, "the President wants you to take out the Black Hand any way you can."

Bolan had gladly agreed to the proposal. Combating groups like the Black Hand was a task for which he was uniquely qualified by virtue of his military background and his subsequent personal campaigns against the Mafia, against those behind the international drug trade and terrorists in general. The chance to go after one of the most feared and deadly terrorist groups in the Middle East fit in with his private agenda.

Little had he realized there would be strings attached, such as having to work with Mehmet Arpinar.

A distant high-pitched whine came from the northeast, growing rapidly louder.

Time to get down to business. Bolan dispensed with the reflection and concentrated on the matter at hand. He reached down to pat the big .44 Desert Eagle on his right hip, then checked to make sure that his 9 mm Beretta 93-R nestled loosely in the shoulder holster under his left arm.

The Turk known as the Fox produced a flashlight from a pants pocket.

Bolan wasn't worried about being spotted. The high grass hid him effectively. As well, his close-fitting combat blacksuit blended perfectly into the surrounding darkness that was only partially alleviated by a quarter moon.

In addition to the M-16 and the handguns, the big man had a pair of utility belts crisscrossing his broad chest, the individual pouches containing spare ammo, garrotes, throwing knives and other weapons of war. In a very literal sense he was a walking arsenal.

The sound of the approaching speedboat indicated it was close to the cove.

The delivery was being made along an isolated stretch on the northern coast of Turkey within two hundred miles of the border with Bulgaria, where the weapons shipment supposedly originated. Certain factions in Bulgaria were notorious as middlemen for the terrorist and smuggling trade.

The Fox pointed the flashlight at the cove and flashed the beam three times. In response the speedboat driver cut back on the throttle and the growl became a rumbling purr.

Again Bolan peered through the scope, surveying the water at the mouth of the cove. A sleek blue craft materialized out of the night, its running lights off, foam gently spraying from the curved bow, and slanted toward the waiting Turks. He counted three men on board, all presumably Bulgarians. He held his fire, patiently waiting for the right moment.

The Fox waved and beckoned the boat closer. He and his men were standing on a level section of sandy shore, and they moved aside so the speedboat could ease nearer and lightly come aground.

A hearty hail in Turkish came from the man at the helm.

The other two men on board jumped into the shallow water the moment the bow touched bottom, lines in their hands, and proceeded to secure the boat by walking inland a dozen feet and tying the ropes to the trunk of a squat tree.

Bolan heard gruff laughter and saw the Fox give one of the Bulgarians a friendly clap on the back. Hefty was talking to the other guy.

The speedboat driver killed the engine and stepped into view, moving to the gunwale. He addressed the Fox, then motioned at the two Bulgarians who had accompanied him. They promptly climbed back on the boat.

The Executioner kept his finger on the trigger. Sooner or later all three gunrunners would get off. He hoped. The M-16 was cocked and ready to fire, the selector set on semiautomatic, the magazine full. All he needed was for his targets to cooperate.

The two Bulgarians reappeared, bearing a heavy crate that they carried to the port side.

While Hefty stood guard, the Fox and the other hardman went to the boat and took hold of the crate as it was lowered to them. They carried the long wooden container to the shore and deposited their burden well above the waterline.

One of the gunrunners vaulted over the gunwale, carrying a crowbar that he handed to the Fox. In a minute the top of the crate was pried off, exposing the contents. The Fox uttered a comment that made everyone laugh.

A regular comedian, Bolan reflected, his body immobile but relaxed. He thought of Arpinar, the government agents, and the chopper crew over two hundred yards to the south behind a hill, waiting for his first shot, the signal for them to enter the fray. Accustomed as he was to primarily working alone, it always felt strange to have a backup. He wryly hoped they wouldn't shoot him by mistake.

In short order the smugglers unloaded two more crates identical in size to the first.

All three gunrunners were back on board. The speedboat driver spoke to the Fox for a bit, then gave a wave and turned. Hefty and the other hardman walked to the tree and began unraveling the line.

Bolan realized the driver had no intention of setting foot off the craft. He decided to take a risk and go for the kill now, while he had a clear shot and before the speedboat put out to the Black Sea again.

The warrior carefully sighted on the driver's head, scarcely breathing as he aligned the cross hairs. Since deviation caused by trajectory was minor up to three hundred yards, he didn't need to elevate the barrel. He simply held his breath, the target dead center in his scope, and caressed the trigger.

With a muzzle velocity of 3,250 feet per second, the 5.56 mm round cored the target's cranium before the sound of the shot reached the others. Struck behind the right ear, the man was propelled toward the stern, his arms flailing, and fell onto the deck.

The crack of the M-16 drew the attention of the three smugglers on the beach. Hefty whipped the SB-30 to his right shoulder and was seeking a target to shoot. The other hardman leveled the M-26, while the Fox merely stood there, his hands empty.

Bolan sent a slug into the Turk's right eye, causing Hefty to twist in a slow, almost graceful pirouette to the ground. He immediately shifted the scope to the Fox's other henchman and fired once more.

The second Turk reacted as if slammed in the forehead with a two-by-four, the impact hurling him from his feet to splash on his back in the water.

Which left the two Bulgarians on the speedboat and the Fox. Bolan ignored the smuggler, training the scope on the gunrunners instead. One of the Bulgarians was going for the wheel while the other produced an AK-47 and commenced firing wildly.

None of the rounds came anywhere near Bolan. He disregarded the gunner and placed the sights squarely on the Bulgarian behind the controls, getting the man in the head just as he started the boat. Convinced the speedboat wasn't going anywhere, the warrior aimed at the gunrunner still chewing up the Turkish countryside with the AK-47 and brought him down.

Six up, five down. A glance to the right showed the Fox to be in high gear, racing along the shore toward a battered brown pickup parked on a gravel road less than fifty yards away. Bolan rose to his knees and looked behind him, annoyed to find no trace of the helicopter and Arpinar. Where the hell was he? It had been Arpinar's idea to spare the Fox, to take the smuggler alive for questioning.

The Executioner stood and moved cautiously toward the speedboat, his gaze darting from body to body on the off chance one of the hardmen might still be alive. None was, and he reached the water without incident.

He examined the contents of the opened crate and found more than a dozen machine guns, submachine guns and assault rifles, all different makes. Some had been manufactured in France, some in the former Czechoslovakia, a few in Belgium and one in Germany. Evidently these particular Bulgarians had operated a far-flung network that extended across Europe.

Bolan pivoted and gazed to the south. There was still no sign of the chopper, one of twenty Huey gunships bought from the U.S. in a recent arms deal. His estimation of his newfound "ally" fell even further.

Forty-nine-year-old Mehmet Arpinar was the director of the Terrorism Department in the Turkish justice ministry's counterterrorism division. According to the background provided by Brognola before Bolan departed the States, Arpinar got his start as a policeman in Istanbul and rose rapidly up the ranks to later become the chief of police in that metropolis. After four years he put in for a spot with the justice ministry and made such an impression that he was later tabbed for the Terrorism post. Brognola had stressed that Arpinar was a good man, a go-getter who preferred to be in the field rather than letting his waist bulge while sitting behind a desk.

The warrior had arrived in Ankara six hours earlier and been met at the airport by the director. He'd instantly sensed a certain reserve in the man, perhaps because Arpinar was being forced to work with Bolan by higher-ups. The idea to team the top American "expert" on terrorism, namely Bolan, with the top Turkish expert had been the brainchild of the American and Turkish presidents.

The Executioner hadn't liked the idea himself when Brognola first told him. He'd only agreed to the proposal because the big Fed had assured him the President was caught between the proverbial rock and a hard place. The American public, rightfully outraged over the slaughter at the embassy, demanded immediate action. The press, true to form, was playing up the attack for every ratings point they could milk out of it. Some so-called experts were urging the President to send in Delta Force despite the fact the elite unit possessed no authority to interfere in internal

Turkish affairs. So the President had compromised and sent in Bolan.

Not that the Executioner's latest mission would become common knowledge. The operation was strictly hush-hush between the American and Turkish governments. Only the two presidents, Brognola and Arpinar knew Bolan's true identity and the reason for his presence in the country.

At that moment the growl of an engine filled the air, only the noise wasn't coming from inland. Bolan stiffened and spun. A second speedboat bore down on him. The informant never said anything about *two* boats. He was standing in the open, exposed to their view, and he quickly took a step toward the knoll, trying to reach cover. But he was too late.

A spotlight hit him, bathing him in its harsh glare, a second before a machine gun chattered and the ground around him erupted in miniature geysers.

2

Bolan knew better than to try to reach the vegetation. He'd be dead before he covered ten yards. Instead he turned and threw himself to the ground in front of the first craft, then rose into a crouch and moved next to the bow.

The firing stopped, but the other speedboat came on rapidly.

As near as the big man could figure, the second boat had to have been a minute or so behind the first. When the driver of the second boat heard the firing, he'd killed his engine and drifted in to take a look. Spotting only one man, perhaps by using a night sight, the Bulgarians had decided to avenge their fallen comrades and take him out.

The Executioner heard the roar of the speedboat's engine grow louder. Small waves lapped at the shore and swirled around his ankles. The strip of beach became brightly illuminated as the spotlight swept right and left. He knew the second craft had to be very close to the first and risked a peek around the starboard side. Bad move.

The machine gunner promptly cut loose.

Jerking backward, the warrior barely evaded being perforated by a swarm of zinging lead that smacked into the side of the boat. He squatted, wood splintering all around him, flying chips striking his hair and his face.

Suddenly the shooting ceased.

Bolan was tired of being an unwilling target. He tensed, then showed himself on the starboard side again to draw their fire, giving them a mere glimpse before ducking in the shelter of the bow. Predictably the machine gunner poured more rounds into the boat.

In a fluid motion Bolan rotated, moving to the port side, and when the gunrunner let up on the trigger he was ready. Rising, the M-16 tucked tight against his shoulder, he saw the Bulgarian manning the machine gun, which had been mounted on the bow, feeding a new ammo belt into the weapon.

Not on your life.

The Executioner squeezed off four shots, every one scoring. The machine gunner snapped rearward, then sprawled over the weapon, his arms dangling lifelessly.

A pair of Bulgarians remained, one at the wheel, the other trying to bring an HK-5 A-3 into play.

Bolan bored two rounds through the gunner's chest, and the man danced backward and went over the side.

Deciding that discretion was the better part of valor, the driver dropped from sight behind the control console and opened the throttle. The speedboat began to swing in a tight loop, making for the Black Sea.

The warrior tried to get a bead on the driver, but the man was nowhere in sight.

In a rush of wind and attended by a muted whine, a Huey swooped out of the heavens, streaking out over the cove, its searchlight coming to rest on the fleeing speedboat. An amplified voice bellowed orders in Turkish and Bulgarian, ordering the driver to stop.

But the gunrunner at the wheel wasn't about to surrender. Perhaps he knew about Turkish prisons, about the infamous cruelty of the guards and the unspeakable atrocities practiced there. It was not without reason that Turkish prisons were widely regarded as hells on earth. Perhaps he decided any fate was better than spending the rest of his life behind bars.

Bolan watched the chopper swing to the east, going around the speedboat and then swinging broadside, exposing the door gunner poised to open up. He ran to the right to remove himself from the line of fire and did so not a second too soon.

The Huey's twin 7.62 mm machine guns thundered to life. Attached side by side on a flexible mount operated by a single gunner, with each gun able to fire between four hundred and five hundred rounds per minute, they made short shrift of the speeding craft.

The warrior saw the Bulgarian thrash and convulse as the heavy slugs tore the man's shattered body to pieces. The speedboat suffered the same fate when the Turk operating the machine guns continued to fire, tearing the control console and the deck into shards. In an awesome display of firepower the twin 7.62 mm guns transformed the boat into a sinking sieve in less than thirty seconds.

Bolan replaced the magazine in his M-16 as the firing ended. The helicopter dipped lower, giving the Turks a chance to inspect their lethal handiwork. He had to hand it to Arpinar. The man certainly knew how to get the job done right.

Banking slightly, the Huey flew slowly toward the shore and hovered over the beached speedboat. The sliding door on the side opposite the gunner opened, and Arpinar stood framed in the doorway, smiling as he surveyed the corpses littering the shore. Like most of his countrymen, he had dark hair and dark eyes. A full mustache rimmed his upper lip. His taste in clothes ran to impeccable suits and polished black shoes, and even on this mission he wore such attire. He looked at Bolan and gestured toward the knoll.

The warrior nodded.

Its rotors whirring loudly, the chopper flew to the knoll and gently settled to the earth.

Bolan sprinted to the aircraft, bending at the waist as he passed under the blades.

"Not a bad night's work, eh?" Arpinar shouted to be heard above the noise of the rotors and the powerful engine. He offered his right hand.

The warrior accepted the help and let himself be pulled up into the cabin. He took a seat beside one of three government agents and glanced at the air force officer doing the piloting.

Arpinar slid the door shut and sat next to Bolan. "After him," he commanded the officer.

Nodding, the Turk at the controls lifted the big copter into the air and angled toward Akcakoca.

"My compliments, Mr. Belasko," Arpinar addressed the warrior using the code name Bolan had selected for this assignment. "You're a man after my own heart. Those sons of bitches deserved what they got."

"You took your sweet time getting there," Bolan said bluntly, concealing his irritation. He was most bothered by the fact that the Fox had escaped. He'd spared the top smuggler at the director's request and by now the man had to be almost to the town. They'd never catch him.

"Perhaps we were a bit tardy," Arpinar responded, "but only because we didn't want the Fox to see us. He wouldn't lead us to where he keeps his illicit stockpile otherwise."

"No one mentioned that part of the plan."

The director adopted a sheepish expression. "If so, the oversight is entirely mine. I thought I made myself clear." He paused and stated sincerely, "If I had known about the second speedboat I would have come to your aid immediately. My apologies. But our informant is to blame, not I."

Bolan saw no reason to press the issue. They were supposed to work together, after all. "So what's next?"

"I have men stationed in Akcakoca. They'll have no difficulty in spotting the Fox, since it's a small town with only one highway passing through the center and very few side streets. If he stops anywhere, they'll radio us. If he keeps going eastward or to the south, we'll know and shadow him. Sooner or later he'll take us to his lair, and we'll have him and his cache of arms."

"And then you and your men will go in," Bolan concluded.

"Not at all. President Mecit has instructed me to give you a free rein and let you handle the dirty work." He paused and looked at the warrior. "That is the correct expression, is it not? Dirty work?"

Bolan nodded.

"Good," Arpinar said, smiling. "My English is a bit rusty and I wasn't certain." He coughed. "English, you know, is taught as a second language in our schools, and most Turks can speak it to varying degrees. It has been a while since last I did so."

"You're doing fine," Bolan told him, and noticed the man seemed genuinely pleased by the compliment. He still didn't know quite what to make of the guy. Arpinar was vain and egotistical, without a doubt, but no more so than others in similar positions of authority whom the Executioner had met in his travels. The crucial question had yet to be answered, though—could Bolan rely on the man in a pinch? If not, he'd sever their partnership at the first opportunity no matter what Brognola or the President wanted.

"May I speak frankly?" Arpinar asked unexpectedly.

"Be my guest."

He leaned toward Bolan and lowered his voice. "I'm telling you this now because I want you to know where I stand and the mistake I made."

"Mistake?"

"Yes. When President Mecit first told me I would be working with an American to try to bring the Black Hand to justice, I expected to be teamed up with a know-it-all type who would try to dictate the course the investigation should take. I resented the idea of Big Brother America meddling in Turkish affairs."

Bolan had to admire the man's honesty if not his sentiments. "The Black Hand might be a Turkish problem," the warrior said, "but they're specifically targeting Americans and American interests in their attacks. That's the reason I was sent in."

"I understand and I sympathize. Those bastards have killed fourteen of your countrymen so far, not counting those they slaughtered at the American Embassy. Ambassador Fleming was most lucky that President Mecit called him in on short notice to discuss the latest development in the Persian Gulf."

Bolan simply nodded.

"Anyway, I was wrong about you. You're not a meddling bureaucrat. And you know how to do a job the way I like to do it. I think we will get along just fine."

"I hope so."

The pilot twisted in his seat and glanced back at them. He addressed Arpinar in their native tongue and tapped the headset he wore.

"The Fox has been spotted," Arpinar translated. "He's turned south toward Duzce."

"Will your agents trail him?"

"That won't be necessary." Arpinar barked instructions to the officer at the controls. Instantly the Huey banked to the south and the pilot killed the navigation lights. "There is very little traffic on the road to Duzce at this time of night. Spotting the Fox will be no problem. We'll follow him ourselves."

Bolan stared out the cockpit window at the murky terrain below. They were flying almost at treetop level, the air force officer handling the big bird with consummate skill. The lights of the town were off to the east. He spied a solitary vehicle moving along a ribbon of roadway, heading southward.

"There he is," Arpinar declared. "After all these years, the Fox is as good as caught."

"I hope you're right about him being able to supply information that could lead us to the Black Hand."

"So am I," Arpiner said. "He's one of the few leads we have at this point. He should be able to since our informant claimed the Fox has sold arms to them in the past."

Still watching the pickup, Bolan asked, "What are the other leads?"

"There are two other avenues of investigation we're pursuing at this time," Arpinar said, nodding at the Fox's vehicle. "One involves the weapons used by the band. Automatic weapons cost much more money in Turkey than they do in your country. Thousands of lira for a single Uzi, for instance. We're trying to discover where the Black Hand acquires the funds for their hardware. They haven't robbed banks, and we know from reliable sources that they don't deal in drugs."

"Someone is bankrolling them?"

"That would be my guess. I suspect there's a sixth member of the band, someone working behind the scenes, as it were, providing them with the money they need. How else can they afford not only their weapons, but their safehouses, the vehicles they rent or buy on occasion, and their clothing and food? If there isn't a sixth person, then I'm at a loss to explain how they do it."

"Have any clues?"

"Nothing concrete, but I'm working on the assumption the sixth member attended the University of

Ankara at the same time as the other five. They were all political science majors, all avid leftists. Unfortunately they let their warped idealism get the better of them."

"Any of their former classmates wealthy?" Bolan inquired.

"You would make a good detective. Yes, a half dozen belong to affluent families, and my men have questioned every one. None of the interviews proved productive, so now my staff has obtained the telephone records for the six in question and is poring over them."

"And what's your other avenue of investigation?"

"One of the gardeners working at the U.S. Embassy vanished the day of the attack and hasn't been back since. A check of his apartment revealed that his personal effects were gone. I believe he supplied the Black Hand with information concerning the regular embassy routine."

"A gardener would have access to such information?"

"You must understand. Working conditions in Turkey are far more informal than in your country. This gardener, Vahdettin, had been employed there for twelve years. He had his run of the embassy and often arrived for work at first light, hours before the American staff. It would have been easy for him to sneak into the secretary's office and copy whatever the Black Hand needed."

"If you're right, the Black Hand might have killed him."

"It's a possibility, but they seldom bother to dispose of those they murder. We would have found Vahdettin's body by now."

A comment from the pilot interrupted their conversation.

Bolan saw the pickup turn off the road onto a drive that wound over a quarter of a mile to a large house situated on a rise.

"We've hit pay dirt," Arpinar stated. "Are you ready for more fun and games, Mr. Belasko?"

3

The Huey touched down in a field several hundred yards north of the house, and Bolan jumped to the ground.

"May God guide your footsteps," Arpinar said, then issued instructions to the pilot.

Crouching, Bolan waited while the helicopter climbed into the sky and disappeared to the northeast. The plan called for the aircraft to circle the house and wait for Bolan's signal. He hefted the M-16 and uncoiled to his full six-foot-three height, then headed across the field and into a stretch of woods.

From a distance the layout of the property had indicated that Bolan had his work cut out for him. At least six acres surrounding the house had been cleared of all vegetation except for a few trees. Approaching the place unseen, even in the dark, would be difficult, especially since there were bound to be guards patrolling the area if the house really was the Fox's base of operations.

The warrior fell into a dogtrot, threading among the thickets and trunks, his senses primed, alertly probing the woods for danger. As it was, he almost missed the flicker of movement to the southeast. The moment he did, he darted behind a tree and knelt.

Someone was coming in his direction.

The big man raised the rifle and used the scope to scan the terrain. He stiffened when he spotted two Turks armed with shotguns, and a large German shepherd. The dog was on a leash held by the older of the men, straining to go faster.

Perimeter guards this far out from the house? Bolan realized Arpinar's plan had worked to perfection and they'd hit the jackpot. The house had to indeed be the Fox's lair, which explained how the smuggler had successfully eluded the authorities for so many years. With the Black Sea such a short distance away, the Fox could unload boats and be back at his base within fifteen minutes, tops.

The two Turks exchanged barely audible words.

Bolan doubted they had seen him. More likely, the dog had heard the chopper and was leading them to the field. Leaning his left shoulder against the smooth trunk for support, he watched them draw nearer. He disliked killing dogs, which were doing only what they were trained for, but sometimes there was no choice.

Since using the M-16 would alert any hardmen at the house, the warrior knew he had to take out the guards swiftly and silently. He eased the Beretta from its shoulder holster. A custom-made silencer fitted to the end of the barrel guaranteed the silent kill he required.

The dog stopped to sniff the air.

Bolan froze. There wasn't much of a breeze in the woods, but there was no discounting the shepherd's keen sense of smell. The slightest gust blowing from him to the dog would send the canine into a frenzy and cause the guards to seek cover.

At a word from its handler, the dog advanced.

Easing back behind the trunk, Bolan placed the M-16 at his feet and assumed a two-handed grip on the 93-R. He estimated the Turks would pass within fifteen feet of his position. If he missed, if he let them get off just one shot, the Fox and any other smugglers at the house would undoubtedly scatter and might well elude Arpinar and his men.

A twig snapped.

The soft crunching of boot soles on the ground enabled Bolan to accurately gauge the guards' progress. When he heard the heavy breathing of the shepherd, he mentally counted to three and went into action.

Both Turks were holding their shotguns in the crooks of their arms when the warrior leaned out and whipped up the Beretta. Without the aid of the sight, the two men were inky shadows. He aimed dead center on the nearest guard, the one handling the dog, and squeezed off two shots. The Turk spun and dropped to the ground, but Bolan hardly noticed. Already he'd shifted the Beretta to the second man, snapping off two more rounds, seeing his target jerk backward and pitch to the earth.

With a fierce growl the dog leaped straight at him.

Bolan glimpsed a streak of motion. The dog was almost on him when he leveled the Beretta and fired a point-blank slug in the animal's barrel chest. But the dog barely slowed. The warrior tried to hurl himself to the right and was off balance when the shepherd plowed into him, knocking him over.

Instinctively the Executioner jammed his left forearm under the dog's jaw as his right hand grabbed for one of the stilettos carried in a snug slit pocket on his skinsuit. The blade sprang clear, and he buried it in the shepherd's neck three times in rapid succession. The dog went limp.

Grunting, the warrior shoved the heavy canine to one side and squatted beside it. His shot must have done the job and sheer reflex kept the beast moving forward. He wiped the stiletto clean and replaced the knife in the appropriate pocket.

Neither of the Turks had uttered a peep.

Bolan retrieved the M-16, then hurriedly reloaded the Beretta and slipped the gun into its holster. He warily stepped to the guards and made sure both were dead before resuming his penetration of the smuggler's estate, moving slower now, not knowing what to expect next.

He traveled almost the length of the woods and spied the grassy tract ringing the house. Halting, he surveyed the property and was rewarded for his prudence by spotting a pair of gunners patrolling the grounds, moving along the tree line, their figures dimly backlit by porch lights at the house two acres away. They wore pants, jackets and caps. Instead of shotguns, this duo packed submachine guns.

Taking the Fox alive promised to be a formidable task. Bolan crouched and moved stealthily closer. The sentries were going from east to west. He drew within ten feet of the open area and flattened, observing the men as they reached the northwest corner and did an about-face.

That was bad news. It meant there were other guards stationed south of the house. Eliminating all of them would take time.

One of the Turks paused to light a cigarette while his companion walked on.

Bolan opened a pouch on one of the utility belts and removed a wire garrote. He crawled to the edge of the woods, stopping at the base of a tree in deep shadows. Laying the rifle at his side, he gripped the slender but sturdy handles at the ends of the garrote and crossed them.

The first guard had his submachine gun cradled loosely in his hands, and he whistled softly as he walked.

Ten feet to the rear, puffing on the cigarette with his weapon slung over his left shoulder, hiked the second Turk.

Timing would be critical. Bolan let the first guard go past. He eased into a crouch, the garrote at his waist, waiting for the smoker to draw abreast of his position and take a single stride eastward. With the speed of a striking panther he slid up behind the sentry, looped the garrote over the man's head and around his neck, and wrenched on the handles while hauling the man off his feet and into the sheltering trees. So quickly was the deed accomplished that the stunned Turk kicked only once before the garrote dug into his throat and choked off his air.

Bolan gritted his teeth, his arm muscles swelling as he pulled on the twin handles, his eyes on the other guard. The man he held dropped the cigarette and began to thrash frantically and to claw uselessly at the wire.

His companion had gone nearly twenty feet.

With a snap of his right leg Bolan drove his knee into the guard's spine at the small of his back and ap-

plied even more pressure. The Turk made low gur-
gling noises, his movements becoming more sluggish
with each second that elapsed.

The other Turk halted.

Bolan gave the garrote a final jerk and slowly sank
to the ground, holding the corpse. He saw the other
man pivot and look around in surprise.

"Evren?"

The warrior relaxed his grip on the handles and let
the man's head drop. He replaced the garrote and drew
a throwing knife.

"Evren?" the Turk repeated, beginning to retrace
his steps.

Staying low, Bolan brought the knife up next to his
right ear. The Turk didn't appear particularly concerned about his buddy's absence. Maybe the guy figured the second man was just taking a leak.

The guard laughed lightly, strolling to the spot
where the warrior had jumped his companion. Then
he stopped and peered into the woods. *"Evren?"* he
called out yet again and added a long comment.

Surging erect, the Executioner flung the knife in an
overhand toss, swinging his body and left leg forward
while his knife arm swung down and out in a smooth
sweep.

In the act of trying to locate his buddy in the trees,
the sentry was still smiling when the blade streaked
from the gloom and caught him at the base of his
throat, slicing all the way in to the handle. He automatically released the submachine gun and clutched at
his ruptured neck, his eyes wide in terror, blood
spurting from his gaping lips. Staggering backward, he
succeeded in yanking the throwing knife out. But in

the process his blood spurted from the hole, a crimson geyser that sprayed over his clothes and the grass. Spinning, he took several paces toward the house, his right arm outstretched as if reaching for help, then abruptly sank to his knees.

Bolan reclaimed the M-16 and moved from cover. He picked up the throwing knife, wiped the blade on the dead guard's jacket, then slid it into its sheath. Time for the main event. The warrior sprinted to a tree dozens of yards away. Stopping behind the trunk, he peered out and studied the Fox's stronghold.

A two-story frame structure, the house was white with black trim and had both a front and back porch. Lights were on in almost every room and shadows flitted across many of the drawn shades. There was no sign of more guards.

Odd, Bolan thought. He wondered why the Fox hadn't given the alarm after returning from the botched operation at the cove, and concluded the smuggler had to believe he'd escaped unscathed yet again from the bumbling authorities. His mistake.

The warrior ran to another tree much closer to the north side of the house. He spotted the pickup parked at the southwest corner. Two other vehicles stood nearby, a brown sedan and an old truck with a canvas-covered bed. Satisfied no one was watching him, he stepped into the open, heading for a third tree.

Without warning, the back door of the house opened and out came a pair of Turks, one carrying a rifle, the other an Uzi. They turned in the Executioner's direction.

Bolan ducked back into cover, crouched and drew the Beretta. The men were conversing; neither had seen him. Were they taking a stroll or were they going to relieve the pair he'd slain? He couldn't let them find the corpses.

The men walked casually northward. They chatted amiably and had no inkling of danger until a grim apparition clad in black materialized in front of them.

The big man fired twice, drilling each Turk through the forehead. Neither uttered a sound before falling to the ground.

Bolan sprinted for the stronghold, holstering the 93-R on the run, scanning the windows for witnesses to his attack. Sooner or later someone was bound to take a look outside and spy the bodies. Consequently he decided to change his tactics. The methodical approach was out of the question. The penetration had to be conducted hard and fast if he wanted to take the smugglers by surprise and capture the Fox.

No alarms sounded, no one shouted out, as the warrior crossed the yard and reached the house. He hugged the wall and listened to soft Turkish music and subdued voices inside. Either the Fox had guests or there were a dozen or more smugglers involved in the operation and they were inside enjoying themselves. Another possibility occurred to him. Maybe they were business associates who had planned to purchase part of the incoming shipment. In any event, they were going down.

Bolan thought of the thousands of weapons the Fox had distributed on the black market over the decade and how many innocent lives had to have been taken by those using the guns. He worked his way around to the rear door, carefully passing beneath each window and treading silently on the porch.

The Executioner stepped to the back door and was reaching for the knob when the door was opened from the inside. There, framed in the doorway, his expression one of total shock, was the Fox.

4

A grizzled brigand whose lined, weathered features were the result of a rough life lived on the raw edge, the Fox recovered his composure in a heartbeat, yelling a warning while clawing for a weapon holstered under his jacket.

Bolan couldn't afford finesse. He smashed the rifle stock into the Turk's face, crushing the smuggler's nose and causing the man to stumble to his knees. The warrior moved aside and glanced down a narrow hallway, spotting a man holding a wine bottle in one hand and a glass in the other. A pistol protruded from his belt.

The gunner let go of both bottle and glass and went for his weapon, but his speed left a lot to be desired. A wreath of 5.56 mm slugs curtailed his effort and punched him backward onto the floor.

Meanwhile the Fox was trying to collect his wits and stand, his hands pressed to his shattered nostrils as he vigorously shook his head.

Bolan grabbed the smuggler by the shoulder and yanked him erect. Hearing shouts erupt within the house, he checked the Fox's hip and found a Luger that he promptly tossed off the porch.

The smuggler tried to seize the M-16 by the barrel, but with a flick of his arms Bolan rammed the rifle into the pit of his adversary's stomach, doubling him over. He gripped the man's collar and backpedaled, pulling the Fox after him, scanning the windows and the doorway for more opponents, ready to cut loose one-handed.

The curtains in the left-hand window parted and a burly man holding an MP-40 submachine gun glared out. A short burst from the M-16 punched him into the room beyond.

The numbers had almost run down. At any moment the place would be crawling with hardmen. The Executioner jumped off the porch, the Fox in tow, and headed toward the woods to the east. If he could outdistance the gunners who were sure to follow, he stood an excellent chance of delivering the smuggler to Arpinar in one piece.

Several men filled the doorway, and the warrior cut loose with the M-16. Two fell, and the third ducked out of sight.

Whirling, his left hand a vise on the Fox's collar that forced him to keep pace, the big man ran for the sanctuary of the forest.

To the south a pair of guards sprinted toward the house.

Trying to keep the Fox alive was a distinct handicap to Bolan. Under different circumstances he would have taken out the smuggler and been done with it. But since there existed a chance that the man could provide critical intel on the Black Hand, and since countless American lives might be saved in the bargain, the Executioner was determined to do whatever it took to keep the man breathing.

Strident yelling at the stronghold heralded the arrival of four gunners.

The Fox muttered something in Turkish.

"Not a word out of you," Bolan snapped, wondering if the man understood English. They were more than twenty-five yards from the house and going strong. Already they'd passed a few trees that partially screened them from their pursuers. Another thirty seconds would give them a comfortable lead.

The hardmen left the porch and fanned out across the grass. One of them spied Bolan and his prisoner and alerted the others.

The chase was on.

A submachine gun burped and rounds dug into the ground on the big man's left.

Twisting, Bolan fired on the run, swinging the M-16 in a semicircle, not really expecting to score but hoping to discourage the eager beavers on his tail.

The smugglers hit the dirt.

The tactic had bought a few precious seconds, and Bolan raced onward. He was surprised the Fox didn't balk, didn't try to slow him down. Maybe the man knew Bolan wouldn't tolerate any resistance. Or, more likely, the Fox was acutely aware he could be struck by a stray round from his own men and knew reaching the trees was to his advantage also.

Random shots rang out but none came close.

At last the Executioner attained the welcomed cover of the murky forest. He shoved the Fox to the ground and growled, "On your stomach and stay put."

The man promptly complied.

Time for the signal, Bolan decided, and pulled the M-18 smoke grenade Arpinar had given him from his left pocket. Used specifically for ground-to-air signaling, the light green cylinders spewed either red, green or yellow smoke for up to a minute and a half. In this case, as indicated by the fact both ends of the M-18 he held were yellow, the smoke would be a bright lemony hue.

From various directions the Fox's band was converging on the warrior's position. Bolan yanked out the safety-pin pull ring and hurled the M-18 as far as he could onto the grass, then dived for cover behind a nearby tree.

Smoke billowed from the canister the instant the grenade hit the earth.

Exasperated shouts greeted the maneuver.

The warrior glanced at the Fox, who was prudently hugging the ground, then pressed his right eye to the hyperminiscope and scanned the tract between the tree line and the house. He fixed the sight on a hardman coming in from the north. A stroke of the trigger brought the gunner crashing down.

Five fireflies seemed to sparkle in the darkness, and a swarm of killer lead zinged into the woods, thudding into trunks, clipping off twigs.

Bolan stayed low, riding out the death storm. When the smugglers expended their ammo he popped up, found a Turk hastily reloading a spent magazine and snapped off three shots that flipped the man onto his back.

A few more figures left the porch and sprinted toward the woods.

If Arpinar didn't get there soon, Bolan would have to move farther into the trees. He spied a third smuggler just as the man stepped from concealment in the yard and leveled a submachine gun. Drawing back, he heard the gun thunder and listened to the slugs peppering the undergrowth.

Suddenly the trees overhead swayed and rustled as the Huey arced down from the stars and hovered. A searchlight stabbed down and caught the gunner in its glare. Instantly the aircraft's twin machine guns drowned out the smuggler's weapon and he jerked in a macabre dance of death before toppling onto his face.

The sight of the gunship apparently spooked most of the hardmen, who disappeared into the trees. Some offered a token resistance, and the Huey went after each one, swooping right and left like a gigantic bird of prey, taking the gunners down one by one.

Straightening, Bolan watched the unequal battle for a second, then stepped to the Fox's side and crouched. "You can get up," he said.

The Turk didn't budge.

Bolan nudged the man's shoulder with the rifle barrel. "You heard me. Get up."

Still no reaction.

Leaning forward, the Executioner saw a dark stain on the Fox's temple and reached down to feel the Turk's neck for a pulse. His probing fingers found only still flesh. Frowning, he realized the Fox had been slain by a random shot from another smuggler. Perfect irony, perhaps, but the man's death left Bolan high and dry where the Black Hand was concerned.

Now what? Bolan mused, swiveling to observe the mopping up operation. They'd lost their main lead. Sooner or later one of the other avenues of investigation might pan out, but Bolan wanted to nail the Black Hand quickly. The summit was coming up, and if the terrorists were still at large the consequences could be appalling.

Brognola had told the warrior about the critically important NATO conference being held in Ankara in eight days. The North Atlantic Council, the chief policy-making body in NATO, was meeting at the prestigious Türkiye Hilton to discuss the latest Mideast crisis. Security would be tighter than a sealed oil drum. The Turkish military was in charge of the arrangements, but Arpinar's department would be working in close liaison with the general in command.

Earlier that evening the director had expressed confidence that the heavy military presence would deter the terrorists from striking. Bolan had kept quiet although he disagreed. To fanatics like those in the Black Hand, the NATO summit was a prize they couldn't afford to pass up. If worse came to worst and he failed to terminate the five members of the band, he'd already agreed to serve as part of the security team the day of the conference. To simplify matters, he was already booked into a plush room at the Hilton, a room he had yet to visit.

The Huey landed and Arpinar's men leaped out. They raced toward the house, their weapons at the ready. The director emerged and strode brazenly toward the tendrils of yellow smoke lingering above the sputtering canister.

"Mr. Belasko?"

The warrior stood and moved from the trees. "Over here."

Smiling broadly, Arpinar jogged to the big man. "So much for the infamous Fox and his band of cutthroats, eh? This will make headlines in every newspaper in Turkey."

"I bet it will."

"My president will be quite pleased," Arpinar stated, and looked around. "Where is he?"

"Dead."

"What? How?"

"One of his own men nailed him."

The irate Turk spewed a string of obscenities. Then he switched to English. "This is bad news."

"Tell me about it."

From inside the house came three shots, followed by muffled shouts.

"Shouldn't we go help your men?" the warrior asked.

"They are quite competent to handle the situation," Arpinar stated testily, thoughtfully scratching his chin. "Where is the Fox's body?"

Bolan showed him and stood by while the director went through the corpse's pockets, removing a wallet and several papers.

"We'll examine these later," Arpinar said, placing the items in his jacket. He headed for the Huey. "We won't waste any more time here, Mr. Belasko. We're needed elsewhere. I'll explain once we're airborne."

As they crossed the lawn and paused near the chopper, one of the government agents emerged from the house and hastened toward them. A short exchange followed between the two Turks.

"There are two bodies inside," Arpinar translated. "Any other members of the band have fled. My men also found dozens of crates and boxes stored in the basement, enough munitions to outfit a small army." He smiled contentedly. "So our trip here hasn't been a total loss."

"But we're no closer to nailing the Black Hand than we were before," Bolan noted.

"Perhaps we are closer than we think," Arpinar said cryptically, then barked orders to the agent who whirled and returned to the stronghold. "My men will handle the mopping up operation here and at the cove. We must fly to Ankara immediately."

"Why?"

Arpinar spoke as he climbed into the Huey. "Two reasons. First, while we were waiting for your signal I received a message from one of my assistants at the ministry in Ankara. Hasan is his name, and he's been examining the phone records of the six wealthy suspects I told you about earlier. He believes he's discovered important evidence."

The warrior joined Arpinar in the copter bay and took a seat. "And what else?"

Motioning for the pilot to lift off, the Turk scowled and looked the big man squarely in the eye. "I'm afraid I have bad news for you, my friend. The Black Hand has struck again."

"Where and when?"

"This afternoon in Izmir, a port city on our west coast. They've abducted a pair of your fellow citizens. It was a classic hit-and-run. A young couple, honeymooners, I believe, were at a sidewalk café on Ataturk Street, which fronts the Gulf of Izmir, when a black sedan roared up and out jumped four members of the Black Hand all armed with automatic weapons. From the descriptions given by witnesses, we think the four were Muzaffer Dora, the leader of the band, and Orhan Mithat, Yeni Yurukoglu, and Nur Yazici. The fifth member, Ahmet Nain, must have been the wheelman.''

"What are the names of the two Americans?''

"Oh. Sorry. Don and Chrissy Hinchey, from Holdrege, Nebraska.''

The warrior's features hardened at the thought of more innocents being victimized by the fanatics.

"Anyway,'' Arpinar went on, "the terrorists fired a few shots to get the patrons to duck down, then Mithat and Yazici grabbed the couple and forced them into the back of the sedan. The entire operation took less than a minute. By the time the proprietor phoned the police the sedan was long gone.''

"Later found abandoned, no doubt.''

"Exactly. Leaving us with no clues, nowhere to turn. Later one of the terrorists phoned an Izmir newspaper and claimed responsibility for the kidnappings. There was also the typical diatribe against the evils of capitalistic, imperialistic, America.''

"Figures. Did the caller make any ransom demands?''

"No,'' Arpinar replied, "and that worries me. I suspect the honeymooners are slated for one of the Black Hand's notorious executions. Five months ago they kidnapped an elderly French couple whose bullet-riddled bodies were later found dumped in an alley in Istanbul." He impulsively punched his right fist into his left palm. "Damn these scum!"

The anger and the distress on the Turk's face were genuine. Bolan realized that here was a man with a passionate devotion to his job. "Do you think the Black Hand is still in Izmir?"

"Yes. They wouldn't have tried to get very far with their hostages. But in a city of three-quarters of a million, finding them is like finding the proverbial needle in a haystack. Every policeman in Izmir has been issued a sheet bearing photographs of the five taken during their university days on the off chance an officer might spot one of them."

The Huey banked to the south and picked up speed.

Bolan digested the latest intel and idly gazed at the machine gunner who was feeding a new ammo belt into the twin guns. "There's something I've been meaning to ask. Why did the terrorists name themselves the Black Hand?"

"The bastards took the name from the title of a book written by a prominent Turkish radical that describes how the black hand of death will crush the life from all capitalists. Although by far their favorite targets have been Americans, they've also killed a few English, Russian and French citizens."

About to turn his gaze forward, Bolan saw the machine gunner suddenly stiffen at the very instant the warrior heard the distinct crackle of automatic weapons fire. The Turk sprawled onto the twin guns, his arms outflung.

The pilot shouted in Turkish and swung the big chopper sharply to the right.

Arpinar bellowed curt directions, then glanced at the Executioner. "We've got a sniper in the trees. Do you know how to operate those machine guns?"

Bolan nodded. Rising, he moved to the machine gunner and eased the man to the floor, then took his place behind the guns. He checked to make certain the selector levers were set on full automatic, opened the bolts on both weapons and took hold of a pistol grip in each hand. His fingers touched the triggers as he surveyed the gloomy expanse of vegetation sweeping past beneath the chopper.

In an abrupt maneuver the pilot dived, bringing the Huey almost down to treetop level. The searchlight speared into the trees, moving in broad strokes from side to side, seeking the sniper.

A muzzle-flash blossomed off to the left and rounds pinged against the side of the chopper within feet of the open bay doors.

Swiveling the machine guns, Bolan was about to open fire when the flash disappeared. He held off, waiting for the smuggler to cut loose again.

The pilot played the searchlight over the area but the sniper had gone to ground.

Bolan surveyed the tangle of tree limbs and brush, trying to detect movement. He felt exposed perched in the doorway and hoped the sniper didn't possess a night sight.

The Huey flew slowly in an S-pattern.

Arpinar unexpectedly stepped up to the big man's right elbow and declared, "I'm not leaving until we get him. If we wipe out the Fox's band, we'll send a strong message to other smugglers and criminals everywhere."

"You should get out of the line of fire," Bolan cautioned.

"What kind of man would I be if I permitted you to risk your life but refused to risk my own?" the Turk responded indignantly.

"Suit yourself," Bolan said, and then ducked as the sniper ripped off a short burst that struck the rim of the door and zinged off into the night.

"There!" Arpinar cried, pointing.

But Bolan had already spied the reddish-orange pinpoint approximately twenty-five yards away. Both machine guns vibrated in his hands as he blasted away. The searchlight illuminated the spot a second later, but the sniper had disappeared.

"Damn." The warrior heard slugs tearing into the undercarriage and held on as the pilot got out of there in a hurry, climbing steeply to the southeast and leveling off.

Arpinar said something to the pilot, who replied curtly.

"The captain is game for another try. Are you?"

"Let's go for it."

At a command from the director, the air force officer dived again, skimming the trees, decelerating until the Huey was barely moving, intentionally striving to draw the sniper's fire. He succeeded.

The Executioner was ready when the muzzle-flash materialized again. Almost in the very same instant he retaliated, the 7.62 mm guns bucking on their mounts, holding the triggers down as he poured it on. Once more the searchlight belatedly revealed the site, only this time the beam caught the sniper full in its glare, showing him jerking on the ground as the heavy slugs drilled into his body.

Bolan let up, staring at the ruptured corpse, and a hand patted him on the back.

"Well done, Mr. Belasko," Arpinar said. "It seems your expertise knows no limits. Do you perhaps have some Turkish blood in you?"

Bolan couldn't help but grin. "Not to my knowledge."

"Surely you must," Arpinar joked, then turned somber. "Now that we've disposed of this problem, we'll proceed directly to Ankara. I'm eager to get on the trail of the Black Hand."

"You and me both."

5

The limousine turned onto a wide avenue bordered by dozens of grand homes owned by Ankara's affluent. Trees lined both sides, and there were few pedestrians.

"We must be very prudent in our questioning," Arpinar said. "The Pamir family is one of the wealthiest and most influential in Turkey. I know the father well. He is a judge on our superior court."

Bolan gazed out the window at the opulent residences. Just minutes earlier they had driven through a poverty-stricken section of the country's capital where the people lived in packed hovels. He adjusted the light jacket he now wore to conceal the Beretta snug under his left arm. "I always find it odd that children of the rich turn to terrorism."

"It seems as if it's often the spoiled children of the wealthy who resent their wealth the most and channel their hatred into social rebellion," Arpinar said. "I have only met the son, Tashin Pamir, twice, and I can't say whether he fits the psychological profile."

"Why didn't you call him into your office instead of driving out to the Pamir home, sir?" asked the director's assistant, Hasan, from the front seat. He sat next to the driver.

Arpinar gave his subordinate a look that would have shriveled a fig. "Didn't you just hear me? The judge and I are friends. I do this out of courtesy for that friendship." He paused. "If you ever hope to move up in rank, my dear Hasan, you must learn tact. Although we are law-enforcement officers our job has political overtones that cannot be denied." He gave a meaningful glance at Bolan.

"I will try to remember that, sir," Hasan said, then coughed nervously. "May I ask you something else?"

"By all means."

"Why have you brought me along? I'm usually stuck in the office and do most of my investigative work over the telephone. Why bring me now?"

Arpinar smiled. "Because you uncovered the information. You have it memorized. Who better to sit in on the interrogation?"

"Thank you, sir."

Bolan detected a servile tone in Hasan's voice. Arpinar, it seemed, intimidated those under him. He'd been moderately surprised to learn the director had a personal limo at his disposal, although, on second thought, he should have expected the perk. It certainly fit in with Arpinar's flashy, if arrogant, style.

The driver slowed as the limousine neared a high wall on the left side of the avenue. He pulled up before a gate and honked twice.

"I phoned ahead to ensure someone would be home," Arpinar said. "Selale, the mother, and Tashin are both in. The judge is on the bench today."

A man in casual clothes appeared and promptly opened the gate, motioning for them to proceed with a wave of his hand.

Bolan glanced right and left as they entered. Meticulously tended lawns and gardens comprised the expansive front lawn. A paved driveway led to a magnificent mansion complete with a fountain in front.

Hasan uttered an exclamation in Turkish, then said in awed English, "I had no idea!"

"Did you think I exaggerated when I stated the Pamir family possesses immense wealth?" Arpinar inquired.

The driver stopped and hopped out to quickly open the director's door.

Dutifully following, Bolan barely suppressed a frown at the turn of events. He was a man of action, a soldier, not a police investigator, and he preferred the direct approach to playing political footsie with suspects. But he was also a man of his word, and he'd given Brognola his promise that he'd do his best to cooperate fully with Arpinar.

An elderly man in a black suit answered the knock on the front door and bowed to Arpinar. He led them down an opulent corridor to glass doors at the rear of the house and indicated two people outside on a patio adjacent to a swimming pool.

Seated in lawn chairs next to a table, sipping tea, were an attractive woman of fifty attired in Western-style slacks and blouse, and a man in his late twenties. They rose as the director exited the house.

Bolan listened as Arpinar and the woman exchanged warm greetings. He surreptitiously studied the son, a skinny guy whose sallow features betrayed the faintest trace of apprehension. Appearances could be deceiving, but Tashin Pamir seemed as formidable as a teddy bear.

"And this is Mr. Belasko," Arpinar said abruptly, turning to him. "He has come all the way from America to assist me in my investigation. Mr. Belasko, may I have the honor of introducing Selale Pamir."

"How do you do, Mr. Belasko," Selale said with a heavy accent. "Welcome to our humble home."

"Thank you," Bolan replied.

Arpinar turned to the son. "And this is Tashin."

The man simply nodded, so Bolan did the same.

Selale and Arpinar conversed in Turkish. The elderly man brought more chairs and everyone sat down.

Bolan sat patiently through polite chitchat, then Arpinar said something that made the mother stiffen and the son lick his lips. In the next breath Arpinar switched to English and addressed Tashin.

"I will repeat it again for the benefit of Mr. Belasko, Tashin." He paused. "When your father learns about your activities he will disown you."

The son began to answer in Turkish, but Arpinar shook his head. Instantly Tashin switched. "I have no idea what you are talking about."

"Come now. Why not save both of us a lot of trouble and confess. I promise I will use my influence to help you."

Selale leaned forward, her hands clenched. "What is the meaning of this?" She glanced at Bolan. "Who is this American? What investigation is he helping you with?"

"My investigation of the Black Hand," Arpinar revealed.

Bolan saw Tashin flinch and make as if to rise, then change his mind.

"What nonsense is this?" Selale demanded. "Am I to understand that you believe there is some connection between my son and that terrorist rabble? The very idea is preposterous."

"Is it? Look at your son's face."

The mother did, her forehead creasing. "Tashin?"

"I deny it, Mother. As you say, the idea is crazy."

Arpinar suddenly rose and jabbed a finger at the son. "Tell your mother about the nine phone calls you have made in the past few days to Izmir."

Tashin laughed. "I have many friends there. What is so strange about that?"

"And I suppose you sent one of these friends twenty thousand lira from your bank account?"

Selale stood. "Twenty thousand lira? Are you certain?"

"Yes. And that's not all. Your son has made regular withdrawals over the past two years of amounts ranging from five to twenty thousand."

"He has his own account," Selale said. "Two years ago my husband opened one for him and deposited one hundred thousand in it."

"There is less than three thousand left."

"What?" Selale blurted, then glanced at Tashin. "How can this be? What have you spent the money on?"

"That is my business," Tashin replied defiantly. He glared at Arpinar. "You had no right prying into my bank transactions."

"I have every right. As soon as I learned about the pattern of phone calls made from this house over a two-year span, I called the bank where I know your father keeps some of his funds and spoke with the bank president. He was most helpful."

"The pig!" Tashin snapped.

Selale touched Arpinar's arm. "What pattern of phone calls do you mean?"

"My office has a detailed file on the Black Hand. We know with a reasonable degree of accuracy where the band has been from month to month since they first formed. There are gaps, of course. But the fact remains that phone calls have been regularly placed from here to cities and towns where the Black Hand was known to have been in hiding, far too often to be mere coincidence. Since I sincerely doubt either your husband or you made the calls, I assume your son did."

"You have no proof of anything," Tashin stated flatly.

"Do you deny knowing any members of the Black Hand?"

"Yes."

"And do you deny attending the University of Ankara at the same time they did and going to many of the same classes?"

Tashin blinked a few times. "Perhaps I did. Is that a crime?"

"I have a mountain of circumstantial evidence implicating you," Arpinar said. "When your father gets home I will present it to him and I guarantee he will agree with me."

"He will laugh in your face," Tashin stated, although his tone lacked conviction.

Arpinar shook his head. "Such a waste. Your whole life ahead of you, and you'll be spending most of it in prison." He folded his arms across his chest.

Bolan could read the emotional turmoil on Tashin's face like a book, and he sensed the guy was on the verge of breaking. He had to hand it to Arpinar; the man was an expert at twisting psychological screws.

"Prison!" Selale said, aghast. "Not our son."

"Aiding and abetting terrorists is a grave offense," Arpinar replied. "Unless he cooperates, I wouldn't be surprised if he's given the stiffest sentence allowed under the law. Ask your husband. He will confirm that our judges always impose the maximum punishment on such offenders."

Tashin Pamir leaped from his chair, whirled and raced off around the pool.

Arpinar glanced at his assistant. "Bring him back."

"Yes, sir."

As Bolan watched, Tashin tripped and fell to his knees. Hasan closed in without drawing a weapon, shouting in Turkish and slowing. He'd almost reached the younger man when Tashin produced a derringer, extended his arm and fired from a range of only two feet. The slug drilled into Hasan's forehead, killing him instantly. He toppled forward as Tashin sprinted for the far wall.

Selale screamed.

An oath exploded from Arpinar and he ran in pursuit.

Bolan wound into high gear, his arms and legs pumping, and passed the director as they rounded the pool. He didn't bother to check Hasan, who was lying on his right side with blood oozing from the neat entry hole. The Beretta swept out in a fluid draw.

"We want him alive!" Arpinar bellowed.

The warrior didn't need the reminder. Tashin could supply critical information concerning the Black Hand. Although his every instinct told him to go for a death shot when confronted by a desperate armed fugitive, he decided to try to wing the man instead.

Tashin started weaving among the trees, using the trunks as cover. He looked back once, and fear etched into his countenance at the sight of the big American with the gun coming on strong. He angled to the left.

Another tree blocked Bolan's view as he was about to snap off a shot. He realized the Turk would reach the wall twenty yards ahead of him and guessed there had to be a gate or a door somewhere nearby. Arpinar yelled behind him.

"I'll get the car and come around to cut him off. Remember, try your best to take him alive!"

Easier said than done, Bolan thought, and spied a narrow door at the southwest corner that stood partly ajar. He brought up the Beretta, striving to aim on the run, but his own motion made precise aiming almost impossible. His finger had yet to stroke the trigger when his quarry yanked the door wide and dashed from view.

He slowed when he came to the doorway, keeping the Beretta level, and peered around the jamb, wary of suffering Hasan's fate. The faint pounding of footsteps convinced him that Tashin would rather flee than fight and he darted into a narrow alley, his gun up and ready, in time to glimpse Tashin Pamir off to the left, turning a corner.

Bolan sprinted to the junction and found a side street. Both vehicle and pedestrian traffic were sparse, and he had no difficulty spotting his quarry a block away. The warrior continued the chase, sticking the Beretta under his jacket and wedging the barrel under his belt. Local police would be inclined to shoot first and question him later if they saw him carrying hardware.

Tashin abruptly halted at another corner, glanced over his shoulder and took a right.

The warrior pounded past a woman and child who regarded him in stunned amazement, then skirted a Turk in a black cap who barked a string of words Bolan couldn't understand. Once at the corner he found himself on the wide avenue fronting the Pamir estate. There was no sign of Tashin.

Puzzled, Bolan looked right and left. The man simply couldn't vanish into thin air. He scanned the walks and the homes lining both sides and glimpsed the bottom half of a leg twenty yards away sliding over the top of a low wall bordering the next house down.

The warrior raced across the side street and peered over the six-foot-high wall to observe Pamir enter a small stand of trees close to a palatial residence. The Turk had to know the neighborhood well, and Bolan couldn't hope to overtake him, but he could outthink the younger man.

He climbed onto the wall and went prone, drawing the Beretta and holding it in a two-handed grip. By twisting at the waist he could cover the trees and the tract of lawn leading to the house. No sooner was he in position than Tashin burst from concealment, racing toward a car parked in the driveway.

Bolan held his breath, steadied his arms and sighted on the Turk's right thigh. His finger curled around the autoloader's trigger, and the 9 mm round drew a cry of pain as Tashin threw his hands in the air and went down.

The warrior rose to a crouch, about to leap to the grass below, when a harsh command in Turkish brought him up short. He glanced over his shoulder and saw two policemen at the corner, their pistols trained on his back.

6

The Executioner froze. One twitch and the police would cut loose. They advanced warily, the officer on the right growling a string of incomprehensible sentences.

Around the corner came the cavalry, the limo's tires screeching, and Mehmet Arpinar was out the door before the vehicle came to a complete stop. He marched over to the policemen, flashed his identification and barked orders sternly, gesturing at Bolan and himself.

The cop on the right argued for all of ten seconds, until the director said something that made him swallow hard and snap to attention, his partner quickly following suit.

Bolan looked at Tashin and saw him hugging his wounded thigh, heard him moaning.

"Did you get him?" Arpinar asked, joining Bolan.

"Right over there," the warrior replied.

"Then let's question him, shall we?"

Bolan went over the side and landed lightly. He kept his finger on the trigger as he ran across the lawn and halted next to the wounded Turk.

Tashin gazed upward, his face contorted in agony, and extended his hands protectively as if to ward off another bullet. "Don't shoot me! I surrender!"

The warrior scoured the ground, found the derringer a few feet away and picked it up.

"You pitiful excuse for a man," Arpinar declared, jogging to a stop beside the younger Turk. "You've brought this on yourself."

Tashin launched into a pleading entreaty in Turkish, but Arpinar cut him off.

"Speak English, fool."

"Please, I'm bleeding to death! I need a doctor right away."

Arpinar studied the blood seeping down Pamir's pants. "Yes, you just might die. What a pity."

"Don't just stand there. Call an ambulance," Tashin begged.

"Not quite yet."

"What?"

"First you will answer a few questions."

"But I'm hurt!"

Arpinar knelt, his right hand sweeping under his jacket to withdraw a Walther P-38. "In a minute you will be dead if you don't tell me what I want to know."

"You wouldn't!"

The older man suddenly jammed the Walther's barrel into Tashin's leg, close to the wound. The guy grabbed his thigh and screamed, the cry becoming a strangled wheeze when the director clamped his left hand on the young Turk's throat.

"You listen to me and listen well. I have been empowered by our president to root out and eliminate terrorist threats to the security of our country. I could shoot you right here and now, put the derringer back in your hand and there would be no repercussions. Do you follow me so far?''

Tashin nodded as best he could, his eyes wide with terror.

''I hope you *do* give me an excuse to shoot you,'' Arpinar went on. ''You've just murdered one of my men, a competent investigator who had a wife and two children, and I'm the one who must bear the bad tidings to them.'' He scowled. ''For that alone you should die.''

Arpinar released his grip on Tashin's neck. ''Now that we have an understanding, I am going to ask you questions and you will answer immediately or die. Are you ready?''

Tashin nodded, tears streaming down his cheeks, and rubbed his throat vigorously.

''You hardly impress me as the revolutionary type. You're a weakling and a coward. Why would someone like you supply funds to the Black Hand?''

The young Turk hesitated until the Walther was pointed at his forehead, then he gasped and blurted out, ''Yeni. Yeni Yurukoglu.''

''What about her?''

''I—I did it for her,'' Tashin confessed.

The director pondered the information for a few seconds, studying Tashin's dejected features. ''You love her, do you?''

''Yes.''

''Let me guess. You met her in one of your classes. She introduced you to her other friends, to Muzaffer and Orhan and the others. Somewhere along the line you bedded her, or thought you did.''

Tashin's head snapped up. "What do you mean by that?"

"Never mind. I want the address of their hideout in Izmir."

"I don't know it."

"Don't lie to me," Arpinar warned gruffly. "They're holding an American couple hostage there, probably at a safehouse. I want the address and I want it now." He placed the barrel against the youth's brow.

"It's 242 Topkapi Street. Apartment nineteen."

Arpinar rose and holstered the Walther. "An ambulance will be here in five minutes. Stay right where you are or else." Pivoting, he motioned for the warrior to join him and headed toward the front gate.

Bolan saw Tashin collapse and begin to cry softly. He shook his head and caught up with Arpinar.

"We needed that address. In an hour we will be on our way to Izmir."

"You took a chance. What if someone had seen you hitting him?"

"Our citizens don't meddle in police affairs."

"He might claim police brutality."

Arpinar arched a brow. "This isn't America, my friend. We don't have your morbid fascination with so-called civil rights. Criminals are not coddled in this country. If Pamir should be stupid enough to lodge a complaint, it would be my word against his. No one would believe him."

"The excitement must have gotten to you."

"Why?"

"You called me your friend."

Arpinar glanced at the warrior and smiled. "You are a man after my own heart, Belasko. Despite my earlier reservations I find myself liking you."

"Here," Bolan said, holding out the derringer. "You'll need this."

"Thank you." Arpinar palmed the gun and cocked his head as the wail of sirens rose in the distance. "I told those policemen to phone my office. Soon my agents will have control of the situation and we can leave. I'll pay a visit to Hasan's family on our way back to the ministry."

"It's rough losing someone under you," Bolan commented.

"Hasan was a fool for not pulling his gun. I'll have a mountain of paperwork to deal with because of him."

The callous remark gave Bolan new insights into his "partner," but he said nothing that would ruin their fragile working relationship. He turned his thoughts to Izmir, to his impending confrontation with the Black Hand, and absently reached under his jacket to touch the Beretta. Payback time was coming up.

THE SUN HAD BEEN below the western horizon for two hours when Bolan finally got the go-ahead. He stood in a house directly across from 242 Topkapi Street, donning an inexpensive overcoat.

"It is all set," Arpinar informed him. "The other tenants have been quietly evacuated from the building under the pretext of a gas leak in the neighborhood. Once you are inside, the police will cordon off the area for a two-block radius."

"Any chance the terrorists have tumbled to the ruse?"

"It's not very likely. The apartments were emptied one at a time. No one has left or entered number nineteen, but a radio is playing inside."

The warrior nodded and glanced around the living room at the half-dozen Turkish police who had entered through the back door shortly after the home was commandeered by the authorities a half hour earlier. The officers were part of a special elite squad, and were armed to the teeth. So, for that matter, was he.

In addition to the Beretta, Bolan now had a Desert Eagle on his right hip and wore a military harness over his civilian clothes. Ammo clips, various grenades, a Ka-bar fighting knife and two throwing knives were stuffed into strategic pouches. Suspended from a shoulder strap under his right arm was a standard Uzi submachine gun.

"President Mecit and Ambassador Fleming have been informed of the situation," Arpinar stated. "Although I don't agree, it has been decided that you alone shall go in. We're to wait fifteen minutes. If we haven't heard from you by then, we'll rush the place."

"Why don't you like the plan?" Bolan asked, glancing at the duffel bag by his feet.

"Because this is Turkish soil and a Turkish problem. But President Mecit sees it differently. Since Americans are being held hostage, he'd rather have an American specialist make the attempt to rescue them. Between you and me, I suspect he's trying to cover himself should something go wrong." Arpinar snorted derisively. "You know how politicians are."

"Do I ever," Bolan said, squatting to secure the top of his duffel bag.

Rising, the Executioner buttoned the middle button on his coat and stepped to a mirror to inspect his appearance. None of the weapons or the harness were visible. Except for a slight bulge under his right arm there was nothing to give him away. In the dark he might even pass for a Turk.

A policeman came up to the director and spoke quickly and crisply.

Arpinar looked at the warrior. "We are ready when you are."

"Give me two minutes to get inside," Bolan said, heading for the rear door.

"Be careful, Belasko," Arpinar cautioned.

"Always." He went through a small kitchen and shoved open a screen door. A narrow walk led to an alley, and taking a right brought him to a side street. Another right took him to Topkapi.

The four-story apartment building was situated in the middle of the block. On both sides were smaller houses. Lights had been left on in many of the apartments, presenting the illusion the tenants were in. Apartment nineteen was on the third floor, on the southeast corner, its two large windows overlooking Topkapi Street.

Bolan bowed his head and strolled nonchalantly across the street to the opposite sidewalk, then moved slowly toward the building. In his mind's eye he reviewed the photographs Arpinar had shown him of the terrorists and those of the American tourists supplied by the U.S. consulate in Izmir.

A portly man walking a small dog appeared ahead.

The warrior slowed and stuck his hands in his pockets. He came abreast of the man almost at the same moment he reached the walk leading to the apartment building.

"Iyi aksamlar," the man said.

Not quite sure what the words meant, Bolan responded with the traditional word for hello. He walked briskly up the walk to the front door and paused to glance over his shoulder.

The friendly dog walker was continuing on and a curtain in the house occupied by the police rustled slightly. Otherwise there was no movement, no other pedestrians or traffic to worry about.

The warrior waited a good ten seconds, giving the man with the dog time to get farther away so the police could whisk him to safety without being spotted from number nineteen. When the man reached the next corner Bolan quickly crossed the threshold and paused to listen. A tomblike silence shrouded the building.

He unbuttoned his overcoat and stepped to the inner door. From his right pocket he drew the master key given to Arpinar by the manager of the apartment building. In another moment he was in a dimly lighted corridor, his back to the wall, his right hand gripping the Uzi under his coat.

Bolan moved to the stairs and ascended cautiously. When he was halfway between the second and third floors he heard the faint sound of music coming from above, a woman crooning a Turkish love song. He crouched just below the landing and scanned the corridor, mentally reviewing the layout of the floor, noting all the doors were closed and the music was now louder.

Apartment nineteen was the last one on the right.

He moved slowly into the hallway, strolling casually toward the far end while reading the numbers painted in white on each door. The music was emanating from number nineteen and had to be the radio Arpinar had mentioned.

As if on cue the radio abruptly went dead.

Bolan still had six feet to cover. He paused, wondering why they had turned it off at that very moment of all times, and saw the knob turning.

The next instant the door was flung wide and out walked one of the terrorists, Nur Yazici.

7

Minutes earlier, at the same time the Executioner departed the house across Topkapi Street, an extremely annoyed Orhan Mithat glanced up from the game of solitaire he was playing at the kitchen table and frowned. From where he sat he could see Nur lying on the living room sofa, her head on a pillow near the end table on which rested the source of his annoyance. "Will you shut that damn thing off!"

Nur opened her eyes and glared him. Then she ran a hand through her short hair and yawned.

"I'm serious," Mithat told her. "I've had all of that crap I can stand."

Swinging her legs to the floor, Nur stared into the bedroom and aligned the shoulder holster she wore under her left arm. Nestled there was a 9 mm Llama compact pistol, the same gun she had once used to terminate a British sailor by cramming the barrel into his mouth and squeezing the trigger until all eight rounds were expended. She rose and went into the kitchen, her lips curled in a smirk. "My dear Orhan, is the music getting on your nerves?"

"It would get on a deaf person's nerves. Turn the radio off or I will."

"And I thought Muzo could be cranky at times."

Scowling, Mithat reached out and tapped the 9 mm Gustav M-45B submachine gun lying on the left side of the table. Manufactured under license in Egypt, large numbers of the reliable weapons were used in the Middle East and in Indonesia, and many had found their way onto the black market. Although not as compact as an Uzi, the M-45B used a box-type magazine that held more rounds. "I can always use extra target practice, and that radio of yours is tempting me."

"You wouldn't dare," Nur responded, moving to the refrigerator. "Your newest toy doesn't have a silencer."

Mithat pointed at the open window. "There are other ways."

"All right. All right," Nur snapped, opening the fridge and examining the meager contents. "I'm hungry and we have nothing to eat."

"So go buy food."

"Why don't you go?"

"I'm busy."

Nur watched him place a black seven on a red eight. "You call playing a stupid card game busy?"

"I don't see you performing brain surgery."

Slamming the door shut, the woman turned and glared at him. "Why must you always treat Yeni and me with such disrespect? Between Ahmet and you it's enough to make us quit the Black Hand."

"There is no quitting for any of us," Mithat said without looking up. "You know that as well as I do."

"Muzo never treats us like you do."

"Of course not. You have Muzo wrapped around your little finger. All you have to do is jiggle a breast and he comes running."

"I'll tell him you said that."

"Go ahead."

Infuriated by her failure to provoke him, Nur stormed into the living room, opened a closet and took out a green jacket. She returned to the kitchen while shrugging into it. "Do you know what your problem is?"

"No, but I'm sure you will be kind enough to tell me."

"You are like most Turkish men. You think you have the right to lord it over all women."

"We do."

"You pig," Nur stated in contempt.

"Don't blame me. It's in the Koran," Mithat said, and quoted, " 'Men are the manager of the affairs of women for that Allah has preferred in bounty one of them over another.' "

"Leave it to you to take a passage from the sacred book out of context."

Mithat finally stared at her. "Who are you to preach to me about the meaning of anything? You are no better, no smarter, than I am. Instead of bickering all the time we should try to get along. After all, our souls will share the same fate."

The reasonable appeal surprised Nur. She studied him for a moment, then spun. "Men! I will never understand them."

"Hurry back. And be careful." He watched her turn into the short hall leading to the door, thinking that he might have been a bit hard on her, then real-

ized she hadn't bothered to switch off the radio.
Peeved, he slapped the cards onto the table, stood and
marched into the living room. He twisted the proper
knob until it almost broke, relishing the sudden silence, then stepped toward the kitchen.

Nur stood with her hand on the doorknob, grinning at him.

He gazed at her, knowing she had deliberately left
the radio on so he would have to turn it off, and despite himself grinned at her deviousness.

With a wink Nur opened the door and stepped into
the corridor.

Mithat was about to return to the kitchen when he
observed her unexpectedly halt in surprise.

"Who are you? What do you want?" Nur asked
someone.

A second later everything blew up. Mithat saw her
grab for the Llama, a flashing draw she had practiced
to perfection. Yet as fast as Nur was, whoever confronted her was much faster, incredibly swift, because her hand just closed on her pistol when an Uzi
chattered and a hail of lead picked her up and
slammed her into the wall.

He bounded into the kitchen and scooped up his
submachine gun, his mind in overdrive. It had to be
the police or the army! And where there was one, there
were many more. He didn't stand a chance alone, and
he wasn't ready yet to become a martyr. The open
window beckoned, providing the only possible avenue of escape from the dozens of officers or soldiers
who were certain to charge into the apartment at any
moment. With the thought came instant action. He
took three strides, slinging the submachine gun over

his left shoulder and bent to ease over the sill. Far below was green grass. To his left, an arm's length from the window, was a downspout, a source of salvation if only it would support his weight.

He slid his body out, gripping the sill with both brawny hands, and let his legs dangle. Carefully gauging the distance, he swung his body once, twice, then, on the outswing, pushed off and desperately lunged for the spout. His fingers clamped onto the metal and his legs banged on the side of the building, but he held fast, swaying, momentarily safe. The spout supports creaked, spurring him to place a foot on either side of the spout and loosen his grip. Down he went.

Mithat grimaced as the friction caused searing pain in his hands. He suppressed the discomfort, thinking of the dismal alternative if he didn't get away. A glance over his shoulder showed the ground racing up to meet him. He increased the pressure of his hands and feet again, trying to brake, but he was still hurtling out of control when he crashed down with a jarring impact, agony lancing his legs, and tumbled backward end over end.

He'd made it! Mithat rose unsteadily to his knees, looked up at the window on the third floor, then heard voices and twisted to discover police officers and a man in a suit emerging from a house across the street. They headed directly toward him.

"Drop your weapon!" the man in the suit ordered, drawing a pistol.

The police were spreading out in a flanking maneuver.

Mithat threw himself forward, flattening and crawling in a mad scramble to the corner of the apartment building. To his rear, automatic weapons chattered and rounds drilled into the turf all around him. Miraculously he reached the building untouched and surged upright, unlimbering the M-45B, listening to their shouts as the police recklessly pursued. If they were expecting him to flee in stark fear, they were in for the shock of their lives.

He counted to two and leaned out, the submachine gun leveled. Three officers and the man in the suit were already on the sidewalk bordering the narrow strip of lawn. Mithat fired, sweeping the barrel from right to left, watching in satisfaction as his slugs punched into their torsos and mowed down all four. But several more poured from the house and rushed up the street.

Whirling, Mithat raced to the rear of the property, leaped over a low wooden fence and dropped into an alley, landing in a crouch.

Two cops entered the mouth of the alley on the west end, running all out.

Mithat knew they hadn't seen him lurking in the shadows, and he nearly laughed at how easy it was to cut them down with a short burst. More would follow, so he stood and sprinted to the east. As he reached the next street he glanced over his shoulder and saw a shadowy form leap from the top of the fence and give chase.

The Turk ran northward, chuckling to himself at the prospect of slaying another fascist. Ahead was a small park he knew quite well, and he had the perfect ambush spot in mind. It was unfortunate about Nur and the operation, but that was water over the dam and now his main priority was to stay alive. And killing the son of a bitch on his tail.

NUR YAZICI WAS DEAD.

Bolan stepped to the right of the doorway and strained his ears to catch the commotion as the other members of the Black Hand reacted to the gunfire. Instead he heard only a soft scuffing noise, then quiet. Inching to the jamb, he peered around the edge and saw a short hallway and part of a living room. But there wasn't a soul in sight.

The silence persisted.

Where was the rest of the gang? He crouched, thinking of the captives, concerned that one of the terrorists might be killing the Hincheys at that very moment. Taking a deep breath, he dashed down the hall and stopped at the corner, swiveling the Uzi the width of the living room.

No one was there.

From his right came a strange noise, a loud thump sounding as if it came from outside the building. He cautiously took a look and found an empty kitchen with playing cards spread out on the table. The window was open.

A noise coming from the bedroom situated directly across the living room drew the warrior's attention. He could see part of the bed, and spied two pair of legs lying side by side, both tied securely at the ankles. In three bounds he was at the doorway and staring down at Don and Chrissy Hinchey. They were very much alive. Loops of rope imprisoned their arms, and gags prevented them from speaking.

The warrior drew his Ka-bar and stepped closer. "I'm an American," he informed them. "You're safe now. I'll have you free in no time." Bending over, he swiftly sliced the ropes binding the husband and started to work on the wife.

Don Hinchey pulled the gag from his mouth. "Thank God you've come! We thought we were goners. Who are you? How did you find us?"

Gunfire erupted suddenly outside.

"Finish untying your wife," Bolan directed, and ran to the kitchen window in time to see Mehmet Arpinar and several policemen bear the brunt of a withering burst that came from the side of the building. The director toppled.

Pivoting, Bolan headed for the corridor. "Stay where you are," he shouted to the Hincheys. "Turkish authorities will be here in a minute." And then he was out the front door and racing to the landing, sheathing the Ka-bar on the run. He took the stairs four at a leap, nearly losing his balance once as he rounded a corner.

As the warrior shoved the outer door wide he heard more automatic weapons fire to the rear of the apartment building. He sprinted to a wooden fence and stared over the top at a pair of bodies sprawled in an alley, policemen according to their uniforms. He glanced left and right and saw a lone figure heading toward the alley mouth.

The Executioner hurdled the fence and went in pursuit.

The man looked back once, his body silhouetted by the light from a nearby streetlight, and kept going.

In that brief moment the figure's stocky profile gave Bolan a clue to the killer's identity. Only one of the Black Hand possessed such a build—Orhan Mithat, by all accounts the number-two man in the gang. He slowed as he neared the street, knowing it would be foolhardy to recklessly expose himself, and warily looked to the left.

Mithat was a block away, just entering a park.

Bolan resumed the chase. Thankfully there were few pedestrians and they were on the opposite sidewalk, gaping in astonishment. Sirens blared in the distance. He wondered where the rest of the police were and realized the risk he was taking in pursuing the terrorist. Any Turkish cop unaware of the situation might mistake him for one of the band and open fire.

The warrior was almost to the park, about to pass a station wagon parked at the curb, when he detected movement next to the trunk of a tall tree forty feet off. Even as his mind registered the motion, a submachine gun opened fire.

8

Bolan dived behind the station wagon. He heard the rounds punch into the side of the vehicle and the shattering of the windows as the glass burst. Crawling forward to the front tire, he paused and waited for the terrorist's gun to run out of ammo.

Moments later the firing ceased.

He rose to a crouch, glanced over the hood at the tree and spied Mithat off to the right, pounding along a narrow path deeper into the nearly deserted park. There were few lampposts along the path. One second the terrorist would be revealed in the pale glow of an overhead bulb and the next he would be concealed in the inky shroud of night.

Bolan continued his pursuit. He wasn't about to fire unless he could be certain of scoring, which meant spraying the Uzi indiscriminately was out of the question. A little closer, though, and he could use the Desert Eagle without having to worry about a bullet accidentally hitting anyone who might be out for an evening stroll.

Mithat abruptly took a sharp left and disappeared around a stand of trees.

The warrior angled to the left also, making for the opposite end of the trees. He expected the terrorist to reappear at some point, but he didn't. Where could he be? Bolan wondered, and the obvious occurred to him at the same instant there was furtive movement *in* the trees and a small, glittering, spherical object came sailing up and out, striking a high limb in the process, barely visible in the gloom.

A grenade!

There was nowhere to go, nowhere to hide. Bolan stretched out on the ground, covered his head with his arms and hoped for the best. He realized that the grenade's trajectory had been thrown off by its striking the limb and knew it would miss him by a wide margin—but by how much?

The grenade went off with a tremendous blast, producing a bright flare of light. Dirt, grass and dust rained out of the sky, peppering the warrior and the surrounding ground.

Bolan hugged the earth, his ears hurting, an acrid scent in his nostrils. His hands and the back of his head stung where clods of dirt and small stones struck them. Blinking and squinting, he looked up and saw the smoking impact crater thirty feet away. Close, but not close enough. He pushed himself up, staying doubled at the waist, and trained the Uzi on the stand of trees.

A short laugh carried to him on the breeze, coming from farther away.

Knowing it was an exercise in futility, Bolan ran to the far side of the trees and sank to his knees, scouring the park and the street beyond. Orhan Mithat had vanished. Round one had ended in a draw, although saving the Hincheys was some consolation.

Sighing, he stood and hurried back toward the apartment building. As he emerged from the park he saw six officers jogging in his direction and took his hand off the Uzi, letting it slide under the overcoat.

One of the policemen spotted him and pointed. All six increased their speed.

Bolan halted next to the station wagon and studied the damage. The vehicle was riddled with holes, the windows were all shot out and both tires on that side had been punctured.

"Mr. Belasko," a short officer declared as the group stopped. "The director says you come quick. He hurts very bad." He paused and gazed at the vehicle. "We heard much shooting and an explosion."

"I tried to catch Mithat," Bolan explained, indicating the park. "The last I saw, he was heading northwest."

The officer barked instructions, and four of the men sprinted for the park.

"Please come, sir," the man said. "Mr. Arpinar say find you. Must hurry."

"Then let's go."

They returned to the scene of the shootout, going around the block instead of cutting through the alley where an ambulance was now parked and attendants were ministering to the pair of policemen who had been shot.

Two more ambulances and nine police vehicles were parked on Topkapi Street, their lights flashing. Officers were everywhere—keeping the curious at bay, going in and out of the apartment building, and scouring the grounds.

Mehmet Arpinar lay on a stretcher near the sidewalk. Three attendants were preparing him for transport to the hospital. He was grimacing in pain, his fists clenched on his chest, but his eyes were alert and roving about the scene. A lopsided grin creased his lips when he saw the warrior approaching. "This is what I get for calling Hasan a fool."

Bolan halted next to the stretcher. "How bad is it?"

"I think I'll live," Arpinar said. "Two slugs caught me in the stomach. It hurts like hell, but there's not much bleeding." He paused and grunted. "I was a bigger fool than Hasan. I tried to take Mithat alive."

"He got away," Bolan disclosed.

"Too bad. I wanted to have the pleasure of feeding him his own testicles."

One of the attendants addressed the director.

"I don't have much time," Arpinar said. "In twenty minutes I'll be on the operating table, and I would imagine I'll be hospitalized for a couple of weeks, at least."

Bolan glanced at the building and saw the Hincheys being escorted outside. An official from the American consulate was with them.

"This is most inconvenient," Arpinar went on clinically, as if discussing an ingrown toenail instead of a gut wound. "I'll be forced to direct our hunt for the terrorists from my hospital bed, leaving you in the lurch."

"Don't worry about me. I'll get by."

Arpinar's features contorted for a few seconds, then relaxed. "I have no doubt you will, Mr. Belasko. But you will need the assistance of someone who can cut corners for you, of a professional in our field. One of my top investigators should have been here by now. My second-in-command has been in Greece the past two days coordinating intelligence material with their secret police. I sent word to Inonu to meet us here—" He stopped speaking and closed his eyes, clenching his teeth against the pain.

The attendants picked up the stretcher and walked toward a waiting ambulance.

Bolan saw a raven-haired woman wearing a blue blazer jacket, a white blouse and gray pleated pants hurry over before the stretcher could be placed inside. An officer tried to bar her path and she flashed identification that made him stiffen and give a smart salute.

Arpinar saw her and they conversed quickly. He did most of the talking while she simply nodded. At one point he nodded toward Bolan. She glanced around, then back again. Moments later the attendants whisked the director into the ambulance.

The woman turned and walked straight toward Bolan. "Mr. Belasko?"

"Yes."

She offered her right hand and gave him a formal smile. "I am Sadria Inonu, deputy director of counterterrorism division. Mehmet has ordered me to work closely with you on the Black Hand investigation."

Trying not to let his surprise show, Bolan shook the proffered hand. "Delighted to meet you."

"I'm afraid I have missed a lot during my absence in Greece. Since the director is hardly in any condition to fill me in, I'm hoping you will do the honors."

"Gladly," Bolan said. "When?"

"There is no time like the present," Sadria replied, and regarded the swirl of activity surrounding them. "But not here. I have a car. If you'd like we can visit a local café. I haven't had a chance to grab a bite to eat and I am starved."

Bolan liked her no-nonsense attitude. He nodded and said, "Sounds fine to me, but first I have to grab my duffel bag."

"Your what?"

"The bag containing my gear. It's in that house."

"Then let's fetch it together."

Bolan led the way. He found the duffel where he'd left it and proceeded to place the Uzi, the Desert Eagle and the utility belts inside. The Beretta stayed in its shoulder holster.

"Do you always travel with enough weapons to conduct a war?" Sadria asked casually.

"Are you kidding? I'm traveling light this trip."

The quip produced no reaction. She thoughtfully studied him, then remarked, "Mehmet informed me that you are an expert on terrorism. For what agency do you work?"

"None."

"You're not a CIA operative?"

"No." Bolan closed the duffel and hoisted it over his left shoulder.

"Then what is your connection to the U.S. government?"

The warrior locked his gaze on hers. "I don't appreciate the third degree. My government and yours have already ironed out the technicalities of my being here."

Sadria frowned. "I did not mean to pry. It's just that I am not very fond of mercenaries."

"Good. Then we should work together just great."

"You're not a mercenary?"

"You're prying again."

"Very well," Sadria said stiffly. "Follow me."

Bolan trailed after her until they reached a car parked a block away. At his request she opened the trunk so he could deposit the duffel inside, then he sat in the front seat and admired the skill with which she threaded through the traffic toward their destination. Since he had to work with her, he decided to mend fences.

"I didn't mean to be so blunt back there. Let's just say that I do a lot of free-lance work for my government."

She glanced at him. "Specializing in terminations, no doubt?"

"Do I detect a note of resentment in your voice?"

"Possibly," Sadria conceded. "Forgive me, Mr. Belasko, but there is something about you, a quality I have seen before. I've only known you a few minutes, but you impress me as being a very dangerous man. There is an air about you. If I had to make a guess, I would say you are a man who, shall we say, disposes of problems for a living."

"Do you have a problem with that?"

"I started my career as a lawyer, Mr. Belasko. A prosecuting attorney, but a lawyer nonetheless. I believe in resolving criminal activities through legal channels, through due process you would call it. There is no one who wants the Black Hand put out of business more than I do, but I would prefer to have them stand trial and be properly punished for their crimes."

"I'll bet Mehmet and you don't always see eye to eye," Bolan commented.

"Not always. The director is a bit too forceful at times for my taste."

"There's a lot to be said for the direct approach."

"An approach you employ regularly, I suspect."

Bolan shifted to face her. "Are you going to be on my case the whole time we're together? If so, I'll save us both a lot of aggravation and go after the Black Hand myself."

A few seconds of strained silence went by.

"I've been ordered to cooperate fully with you, and this I will do no matter what my personal feelings might be," Sadria said.

"I feel better already."

"Sarcasm, Mr. Belasko, hardly becomes anyone."

"Call me Mike. And if I'm being sarcastic it's only because since I arrived in your country I've had to contend with so-called allies who would rather I'd never shown my face. We're supposed to be on the same side."

"We are, but you must bear in mind that this arrangement has been forced on us over our objections."

"I know. Mehmet told me the same thing," Bolan said.

"Then please bear with us."

"I'm trying, lady."

"Call me Sadria."

Moments later she wheeled into a parking space along the curb in front of a small open-air restaurant and climbed out. A dozen tables were spread out in four equal rows. She went to the row farthest from the street and sat at a corner table.

Out of habit Bolan positioned his chair so that he sat with his back to the wall, giving him an unobstructed view in all directions.

"Are you hungry?" Sadria inquired.

"Come to think of it, I am."

"What would you like? I've eaten here before and can highly recommend their seafood."

"Seafood, then, and coffee."

A waiter approached and Sadria ordered for both of them. Then she stood. "Now, if you'll excuse me, I need to use the telephone and contact our office in Ankara to let them know where we are in case something should develop."

She turned and entered the restaurant proper.

Leaning back, Bolan reflected on the events since his arrival in Turkey. Nothing had gone right yet. His hosts didn't want him there, the terrorists were still operational, and he didn't have a clue as to how to proceed. Truth to tell, he'd much rather go after the Black Hand on his own and forget about cooperating with officials who obviously wished he'd dry up and blow away.

Sadria Inonu unexpectedly came through the door in a rush and stepped to the table. "We are in luck. This is good news."

"What is?"

"Did Mehmet tell you about a certain gardener who worked at the U.S. Embassy in Ankara?"

"The one who up and disappeared?"

"Yes. Two of our men have tracked him down. Apparently he took a bus out of the city and fled to Usak, his home town."

"Where is he now?"

"In Usak. Our agents are holding him there until we arrive," Sadria said.

"Why not just take him back to Ankara?" Bolan asked.

"Because Usak is only one hundred and twenty-five miles west of Izmir. If we leave now and take E23, we can be there in slightly over two hours. The sooner we question him, the better it would be. Do you agree?"

"I do, but I also think it would be wiser to take a helicopter instead of driving all the way there," Bolan noted.

"Flying into the mountains at night is dangerous."

"Okay. When do we leave?"

"Immediately. I took the liberty of canceling our order."

"Then let's hit the road."

9

After filling the gas tank Sadria drove to E23, the main artery connecting the exotic port city to central Turkey, and soon accelerated to a steady speed of eighty miles an hour.

Bolan stared out his window at the dark countryside flashing past and tried not to dwell on the fact that Turkey had one of the highest accident rates in the world.

"You've been very quiet, Mr. Belasko," Sadria said.

"Mike."

"Very well, Mike. Since we have two hours to kill, what would you like to talk about?"

"I'm not much of a talker."

"Are you married?"

The warrior glanced at her. "No. You?"

"No," Sadria answered, her full lips curling downward. "I put my career ahead of my personal life and paid a terrible price."

The brutally honest statement prompted Bolan to think of the family he would never have, of the wife and kids he would never know, of the happiness he was depriving himself of in order to fulfill his quest of making the world a better place for his fellow man. Like the knights of the Round Table who had devoted their lives to tracking down the Holy Grail, he'd devoted his life to tracking down those unholy drug lords, Mafia kingpins and terrorists who were responsible for transforming the American dream into the American nightmare and who, in their own vile way, were polluting the world far worse than any ecological disaster ever could.

"We all have prices to pay," he commented. "Some are higher than others."

"Is that the voice of experience speaking?"

"More or less."

Sadria rubbed the back of her neck and suppressed a yawn. "You're right, of course. For any professional woman in Turkey the going is very rough. While legally we have equal rights, women here don't enjoy the same advantages as women in the United States. There are fewer opportunities, and those women who do try to make it must work twice as hard as their male counterparts to make the same impression. It's not fair."

"No one ever claimed life would be fair."

"I know. But when I think of all I've gone through to get where I am today, all the condescending attitudes I've had to tolerate and the constant need to prove myself, I become very angry."

The warrior studied her. "Anger can be good or bad depending on how its channeled. I like to think that I use my anger constructively."

"What do you have to be angry about?"

"A lot. Every time I read about known drug dealers, those who push their poison to ten- and twelve-year-olds on street corners and at schools, getting off with a slap on the wrist, I get angry. Every time I hear about a drive-by shooting in which a dozen bystanders are caught in the cross fire, I get angry. And when I see in the paper that a notorious Mafia capo has escaped conviction on a technicality, I get damned angry.''

Sadria had listened attentively. Now she gave him a quizzical look. ''You are a man of principle. I didn't expect that.''

''You just figured I'm your basic Neanderthal.''

''Not at all,'' Sadria replied defensively. ''There is simply more to you than meets the eye.''

Bolan gazed through the windshield at a small farmer's cart being pulled by a donkey. They streaked past and he glimpsed a weary face lined with the labor of many years turned toward them.

The miles went by quickly. E23 wound through a series of progressively higher hills as it neared the mountains bordering the Anatolian plateau. On both sides lay land tilled for centuries by generations of poor peasants who barely eked out a living.

''It's like entering a whole new world out here,'' Sadria commented at one point. ''Life in the country is as different from life in the cities as night is from day. I was born and raised in Ankara, and I've never been able to understand how these poor people live the way they do.'' She paused. ''Although, when you think about it, there is one advantage to living in a rural village.''

''What's that?'' Bolan asked.

''A longer life expectancy. You never hear of terrorists killing simple villagers. They tend to concentrate their activities in the larger cities. There's more publicity that way, I guess.''

"Maybe so," Bolan conceded. "But I'm sure terrorists wouldn't hesitate to kill anyone, anywhere, if they had a good enough reason."

EIGHTY MILES FARTHER EAST on the same highway, a sedan was fast approaching Usak. At the wheel sat Ahmet Nain, his gaze glued to the treacherous, constantly curving road. "I still think this is a waste of our time," he complained yet again.

Seated across from him, Muzaffer "Muzo" Dora frowned and angrily slapped the dashboard. "If I hear you gripe about this just once more, Ahmet, I'll kick you out and you can walk all the way back to Izmir."

"I would rather be in Izmir than here. We're taking too great a risk."

"What risk?" Dora countered. "The American pigs are safely tucked away. Orhan and Nur will take good care of them."

"That isn't the risk I am talking about and you know it. It's stupid for us to be way out here in the middle of nowhere. There are too many things that can go wrong."

"Such as?"

"Such as our car breaking down or developing a flat. Getting it repaired would be next to impossible."

"So? We'll hike to a phone and call for a tow. Or we can hitchhike back to Izmir."

"And what if we're recognized? Every newspaper in the country has plastered our pictures on its front page at one time or another. I bet every man and woman in Turkey knows what we look like."

Dora snorted. "And has anyone recognized us yet?"

"No, but anonymity is easier to maintain in the cities, and until now we've been smart enough to stay there."

From the back seat came a scornful, feminine laugh. "Working with explosives for so long has turned you into a nervous wreck, Ahmet."

Ahmet Nain glanced in the rearview mirror. "You would be nervous, too, Yeni, if you had half a brain in your head."

"That's enough!" Dora snapped. "We're comrades in the revolution against capitalist imperialism. We mustn't bicker like children. First and foremost is the cause. Our petty concerns must be put aside."

"Spare me the ideological garbage."

Dora looked sharply at his companion. "Since when have you taken to describing our cause in such unflattering terms?"

"Since I began to wonder if there is more to life than hiding out like rats and accomplishing next to nothing."

Leaning back, Dora pursed his lips and traced his left index finger along his facial scar. "I had no idea you felt this way. Why have you not mentioned it before?"

"Probably because I wasn't upset enough to get up the courage."

"Perhaps you'd care to elaborate."

Nain studiously avoided looking at Dora as he spoke. "For two years now we have been trying to overthrow the present government. We've killed scores of people, American scum and others, and bombed dozens of buildings. And what have we accomplished? What do we have to show for all this effort, for all our sacrifices? I'll tell you what. Absolutely nothing."

"In other words you believe we have been wasting our time."

"Precisely."

"My dear Ahmet, think for a moment. When you climb stairs you go up them one step at a time. The same is true for us. We must always bear in mind that we accomplish our goal one small step at a time. But the important thing is to never lose sight of the goal. Casting off the imperialist yoke won't be easy. There will be many years of struggle before it happens and we might not be the ones who live to see it. One day, though, Turkey will be truly rid of all foreign influences."

"And become the ideal Marxist country," Nain said bitterly.

"Yes. What is wrong with that?"

"Everything. In case you haven't noticed, the rest of the world no longer agrees with us. Russia is no longer Marxist. Eastern Europe has cast off communism. Who else is left? China? Now there's an inspiring example."

"You no longer believe in communism?"

"Let's just say I'm having my doubts."

Dora glanced out the window so that his companion wouldn't see his features harden. "This is most upsetting. I wish you'd told me sooner."

"What does it matter?"

"Any chain is only as strong as its weakest link," Dora noted philosophically. "When we first banded together we were filled with resolve. We saw the problem clearly and recognized the solution. Do you re-member?''

"Of course. The problem was twofold—how to re-move all imperialist influence from Turkey and turn the country into a Communist bastion.''

"And the solution?''

"To draw attention to the plight of the masses by attacking U.S. and other capitalist interests wherever we found them. Once the people knew they were be-ing used as economic fodder, they would rise in re-volt.''

"Exactly.''

Nain took his eyes from the road to stare at his friend. "It will never happen, Muzo.''

"And why is that?''

"Because the people don't see themselves as op-pressed and they never will. Because communism is a failure and will never be revived. We have wasted our lives for nothing.''

A minute went by and no one spoke.

"I'm disappointed, Ahmet,'' Dora said, still gaz-ing out the window. "So very disappointed.''

"I knew you would be upset.''

"And you've felt this way for some time?''

"Oh, four or five months. I almost spoke up after our botched attack on the American embassy. Killing Marines I could understand, but killing those women was so senseless.''

Dora finally turned toward the younger man. "You've never objected to eliminating women be-fore.''

"I know. Maybe my conscience has caught up with me,'' Nain said, and laughed.

"You always were softer than the rest of us."

"What's that supposed to mean?"

"Nothing, my friend," Dora said, smiling to show he meant no offense. "Tell me. What do you propose to do now?"

Encouraged by the smile, Nain became bold enough to reply. "I've been thinking of taking time off, of traveling to Europe for a few months to regain my perspective."

Yeni leaned forward, her long hair spilling over the top of the front seat. "But you're our explosives expert. How will we get by without you?"

"You can manage for a while."

"We took an oath, remember?" Yeni reminded him. "We would stick together always until our goal was accomplished or we were six feet under."

"I remember it vividly. I wrote it, if you'll recall. That was an eternity ago, Yeni, and I'm not the same person I was back then. None of us are."

"But you can't just—" Yeni started to protest.

Dora cut her off. "If he wants to take time off, it's his prerogative. We won't stand in his way."

Nain glanced at him. "Do you mean that?"

"Of course."

"What a relief. I expected you to fly into a rage and order me to stay."

"I know a lost cause when I see one," Dora stated. "I just hope you will help us take care of Vahdettin."

"If you insist. But I agree with Orhan. Taking this gardener out is unnecessary."

"Humor me. Do your part and after we return to Izmir you can leave for Europe."

"You mean it?"

"Have I ever lied to you?"

"No."

"Then don't insult me again," Dora said sternly. His mood abruptly changed and he grinned, rubbing his hands in anticipation. "We will teach Vahdettin the folly of double-crossing the Black Hand. He'll serve as an example to others who might entertain similar ideas."

"Orhan says the gardener might not have deliberately deceived us," Ahmet noted. "Orhan says there could have been circumstances beyond Vahdettin's control."

"Orhan talks too much," Dora said. "What does it matter whether we were tricked or not? Vahdettin took our money, didn't he? And the information he provided turned out to be incorrect. He knew the terms of our arrangement. Ten thousand lira for the ambassador's schedule. An accurate schedule. As it turned out, we came across as incompetent fools."

"We'll be even bigger fools if it turns out he's not in Usak."

"Where else would he go?" Dora countered. "He mentioned to Nur once that he was born there. It's the most logical place for him to hide from our retribution. But as he is about to discover, there's no hiding from the Black Hand."

"Let's get this over with quickly," Nain said. "I can't wait to leave for Europe."

"Patience, my friend. Once the gardener is disposed of, you will have all the free time in the world," Dora assured him, and cast a meaningful, somber glance at Yeni.

10

Sadria slowed to the speed limit as they entered the town of Usak and was unable to suppress a yawn. "At last," she commented.

"You should have let me drive part of the way," Bolan said. The drive through the mountains had been an endurance test of nerves and stamina and she had maintained a steady, fast pace.

"I'm fine."

"Where are your agents holding the gardener?" Bolan inquired.

"At the police station. They found him at his brother's and the family put up quite a fuss. Our men felt it wise to keep him in protective custody until we arrived." Sadria began checking street signs.

E23 formed a junction at the center of the town with another major artery running north and south. Mainly businesses lined both sides of the highway.

Continuing eastward for two more blocks, Sadria suddenly braked and pulled over. "This is the station."

Bolan followed her into a two-story building of recent construction. Inside was a waiting area and a counter where a burly officer stood writing a report. He glanced up, his eyes narrowing.

"Iyi aksamlar."

Sadria addressed him formally and flashed her identification. The officer dropped his pen instantly and escorted them to an office where two men in suits were seated chatting with a lieutenant. The men greeted Sadria warmly.

Bolan was introduced to the agents, Habab and Tikrit, then stood next to the wall while the Turks went on at length in their own language. Finally Sadria motioned and he went with them down a flight of stairs to the holding cells. In one of them sat a forlorn elderly man wearing a blue coat, a pair of dark, loose breeches, a white shirt and a blue cap.

Sadria and the agents entered the cell and she began earnestly questioning Vahdettin. He answered readily enough, and after a few minutes she turned to the warrior. "We're in luck. He admits to helping the Black Hand. They paid him ten thousand lira for a copy of the ambassador's schedule. He never intended to give up his job, but after the raid he became afraid someone would discover the part he played so he came here."

"Does he speak English?" Bolan asked, hoping to interrogate the man himself.

"No. I'll gladly translate for you."

"Does he know where we can find the Black Hand right now? Do they have a place they use frequently to hide out?"

"I already asked him and he has no idea. They told him very little about their operation."

"Figures," Bolan said. He didn't bother to add that this trip would probably turn out to be a bust.

Sadria studied his features, then unexpectedly inquired, "Are you still hungry?"

"I can hold out."

"But I'm famished. There's a tavern right around the corner. We can take a thirty-minute break and come back."

"Whatever you want."

The agents listened while Sadria explained. "Tikrit and Habab will stay here until we return," she stated, walking from the cell, and said nothing else until they were standing on the sidewalk outside. "Okay, Mr. Belasko. What's bothering you?"

"What makes you think something is?" Bolan parried.

"Because I watched your eyes in the lieutenant's office and again downstairs. You're upset and I would like to know the reason."

"Let's just say I'm champing at the bit."

"I'm sorry. I don't know that expression."

"I'll explain over a beer."

They walked to the tavern. A dozen patrons were seated at tables, a few standing at a counter. Bolan moved to a corner and took a seat, conscious of the stares directed their way.

"You must forgive them," Sadria said. "They don't see many strangers here."

A man came from around the counter, wiping his hand on his apron, and casually approached their table.

Bolan folded his hands on the tabletop and idly listened to Sadria and the man converse. She turned to him after a minute.

"There isn't much of a selection, I'm afraid. He has pilaf, which is rice fixed with onions, currants and pine nuts, or lamb chops. Which would you like?"

"The lamb sounds good."

"And to drink?"

"Tuborg."

Sadria gave the order and waited until the man was gone before casting a critical gaze at the warrior and saying, "Okay. If you don't mind, I'd like to know what is bothering you."

So Bolan told her.

"STOP THE CAR!" Dora barked. "This is the address."

Nain brought their sedan to a lurching halt and glanced out his window at the dwelling thirty feet from the side of the secondary road. "Are you sure this is the place?"

"If the man at the market told us the truth, it's where Vahdettin's brother lives," Dora responded testily, opening his door. "Yeni, you come with me. A pretty face can often pry open sealed lips."

"As you wish."

Dora slid out and made certain the Bernardelli PO 18 pistol was tucked securely under his belt and hidden by the flap of his lightweight blue jacket. He waited for Yeni to emerge, then slammed the door and headed for the house.

"What's troubling you?" Yeni asked.

"This is taking too long," Dora answered. Much longer than he'd anticipated. But how was he to know tracking down Vahdettin would be so difficult? He'd forgotten that many of those living in rural areas didn't possess phones, thereby eliminating the phone book as a means of locating the gardner's relatives. They'd been forced to conduct their hunt the hard way, by stopping at every store and tavern they found and making inquiries without arousing suspicion. More than an hour had been wasted before they hit the jackpot.

Turgut Vahdettin's residence was a simple mud-washed one-story affair typical of those lining the dusty road. Dim light rimmed the crude curtains covering both front windows.

Dora strode to the wooden door and heard voices within. He knocked lightly twice and smiled, wanting to make a good impression on whoever answered.

Yeni stood on his right.

The voices inside ceased and someone called out, "Who is it?"

Twisting, Dora nodded at Yeni.

"Pardon us, sir, but is this the Vahdettin house?" she asked dutifully.

"It is. What do you want? It's late."

"We would like to have a word with you, if you please."

"What about?" the man demanded gruffly.

"If you are Turgut Vahdettin, we would like to talk about your older brother, Ismet."

The door swung open and a stocky, muscular man in his forties regarded both of them suspiciously. "I'm Turgut. Are you with the police?"

"No, sir," Yeni answered. "Why would we be police officers?"

"Because they took Ismet away early this evening," Turgut said. "Two officers and two men from the ministry hauled him off. They said we could visit him at the station for the next few hours, but my wife won't let me go.'' He paused. "If you're not with the police, then who are you?''

"Friends of your brother's,'' Dora stated, and started to leave. They'd learned what they needed. If the police had the gardener, then they'd have to visit the police station.

"Wait a minute,'' Turgut said. "How do you know my brother?''

"We met him in Ankara,'' Yeni replied. "I work as a clerk at the American Embassy.''

"And he told you about me and where I live?''

"We were good friends,'' Yeni declared sweetly.

Dora saw the man's eyes flick from him to her and abruptly widen, as if in dawning recognition.

"Oh. I see. Well, thanks for stopping,'' Turgut said, and began to close the door.

In one stride Dora had his foot pressed against the bottom of the door, preventing it from shutting, and his hand on the Bernardelli. "Don't you want to know our names so you can tell Ismet when next you see him?''

Turgut's face betrayed a trace of fear as he swallowed and said, "Yes. Of course. How thoughtless of me. What are your names?''

"I believe you already know,'' Dora said bluntly.

Suddenly Turgut whirled and ran, shouting a warning to whoever was inside. "They're here! The Black Ha—''

The silencer-equipped Bernardelli swept up and out and Dora stroked the trigger twice, drilling two holes in the back of Turgut's head. The man went down, crumpling soundlessly to the floor.

"Turgut?" a woman called out.

Dora gazed down the narrow hallway and saw a neatly dressed, heavyset woman step into view. The man's wife, no doubt. She gaped at her dead husband and opened her mouth to scream. Before she could alert the whole neighborhood he fired a round into the center of the circle formed by her full lips. She staggered backward, her arms flailing, before collapsing to the floor.

Two down. Were there any more? Muzo wondered. He hurried forward and found a living room and an attached kitchen. There were two doors on his right, one open, one closed. Shoving the first wide he discovered an empty bedroom. As he went to grab the knob on the second door it unexpectedly swung inward.

A young man of about twenty stood there. "Who are you?" he demanded. "Where are my parents?"

"In paradise, and you should join them," Dora replied. He smiled, touched the silencer to the startled youth's forehead, and fired.

"Was that necessary?"

Dora spun to find Yeni regarding him critically. "The fool of a father recognized us. What else was I to do? He would have contacted the authorities."

Yeni leaned to the right and stared at the young man's naked feet. "You didn't need to kill him. You could have slugged him."

Anger welled in Dora and he almost slapped her face. "Is everyone becoming soft but me? You know the rules. Never leave a witness." He strode past her and out the front door, wedging the pistol under his belt.

"What now?" Yeni asked, catching up with him.

"Use your pitiful excuse for a mind. The police took Ismet to the Usak station. He might still be there," Dora said, crossing the strip of yard to the car.

"Surely you're not thinking of attacking a police station?"

"Why not?" Dora rejoined, going around to the passenger side and climbing in.

"What happened?" Nain asked anxiously. "I saw you shoot that man."

"So?" Dora snapped. "He was nothing but an ignorant peasant."

Yeni got in the back, her lips compressed, and slammed the door.

"Drive," Dora directed. He took out the pistol and began to reload. His hands were steady as they ever were. A twinge in his right shoulder reminded him that his wound was not yet healed.

"Where am I driving to?" Nain inquired as he accelerated rapidly.

"We must find the police station."

Nain glanced over his shoulder at Yeni, then at their leader. "Why?"

"Because I say so."

Yeni snorted. "Tell him the truth. Tell him you intend to barge into the station with your guns blazing."

"I never said any such thing," Dora growled, glaring at both of them. "And frankly, I'm growing tired of having my orders questioned. Years ago you both agreed that I should be the head of our organization.

You both agreed to follow my directions at all times. Why, now, are you both being such pains in the ass?"

"What is this about the police station?" Nain asked, ignoring the question.

"Two fascists from the ministry took Vahdettin there."

"Agents from Arpinar's office?"

"Most likely," Dora replied. "Do you remember that article we saw in the newspaper on the illustrious director of counterterrorism division? The one where he claimed he would have us all in custody or in the morgue within the next twelve months?"

"Yes."

"How embarrassing do you think it would be for him if a pair of his precious agents were slain by the infamous Black Hand?"

Nain blinked a few times. "Are you serious?"

"Never more so. We have everything we need in the trunk."

"But a police station!"

Dora nodded. "There can't be more than ten or twelve officers in a town this size, and many of them are off duty at this time of night. Country cops like these carry pistols, and pistols are no match for Uzis, AK-47s and plastique, eh? This is a marvelous opportunity. We'll make headlines all over, and Arpinar will be left with egg on his face."

"Provided we survive," Nain said softly.

"Cheer up," Dora stated. "We all die sooner or later. Why not go out in style?"

11

Bolan and Sadria walked slowly back to the station. The meal had served to further reduce the tension between them. As they neared the corner, Sadria reached out and touched his hand.

"Thank you."

"For what?"

"For the most pleasant sixty minutes I've enjoyed in ages. It's so rare that I get any time to relax anymore. I treasure these moments."

"Your agents are liable to be wondering where we went. Didn't you tell them we'd be back in half an hour?" Bolan reminded her.

Sadria chuckled. "Let them wonder. Superiority has its privileges."

They rounded the corner. A cool breeze blew in from the northwest, caressing their faces.

"Since you were so honest with me, may I return the favor?" Sadria asked.

"Be my guest."

"I like you, Mike. My initial impression of you was wrong. You don't have the air of a cold-blooded mercenary."

Bolan said nothing and she went on.

"You're not like most men I know. You're very frank, very open. You don't puff yourself up and pretend to be something you're not. I admire such a trait."

Why was she flattering him? Bolan wondered. He considered the obvious and discarded the notion, but the next moment she touched his hand again, letting her fingers trail along his skin for several heartbeats.

Sadria cleared her throat and faced forward. "Back to business. I doubt whether Ismet Vahdettin knows anything of importance, but we must go through the motions of interrogating him."

The same burly officer stood at the counter. He smiled at Sadria but gave Bolan a cold stare.

Habab and Tikrit were waiting impatiently at the top of the stairs. Tikrit, the leaner of the duo, addressed her rather gruffly and received a stern rebuke. The agents then led the way to the cell.

Vahdettin was pacing back and forth, his hands behind his back, his anxiety transparent.

"Are there any specific points you want me to bring up?" Sadria asked the warrior.

"No. I'll leave the questioning in your capable hands."

"Thank you."

Bolan folded his arms across his chest, leaned on the bars and watched the interrogation unfold. The Turkish agents used a variation of the standard good-cop bad-cop routine, with Habab and Tikrit playing the part of the hard-asses and Sadria acting as the angel of mercy. They gave the gardener the third degree, and after half an hour Vahdettin was sweating profusely and repeatedly mopping his brow.

Sadria joined the warrior and sighed. "We've learned a lot, but none of it is very useful. Apparently the Black Hand had the embassy under surveillance for a while, keeping track of the comings and goings until they identified the employees. It was Orhan Mithat and Nur Yazici who first approached Ismet and offered to pay him ten thousand American dollars in exchange for certain information. He claims he initially refused."

"Do you believe him?"

"Yes. He has no criminal record. Basically he's an honest, hardworking man who let greed get the better of him. He said he considered notifying the authorities after the pair contacted him, but Mithat had made it clear that if he did the Black Hand would track down his relatives and murder them."

"Typical," Bolan said harshly.

"So poor Ismet caved in. He agreed to obtain a copy of the ambassador's schedule. They never told him the reason they wanted it and he never asked."

"He must have suspected."

"Oh, yes. But receiving a lot of money for a dirty deed can soothe any conscience. I gather he thought they would assassinate the ambassador. Never in a million years did he expect them to launch an all-out attack on the embassy. He became terrified of being implicated as an accomplice so he fled here, thinking he could stay with his brother and live off his windfall."

"Ten thousand doesn't go very far nowadays," the big man remarked.

"In America perhaps not, but in Turkey ten thousand goes a long way. Our standard of living is much lower than yours. A man Vahdettin's age could live quite comfortably for the rest of his life on such a sum."

"Where's the money now?"

Sadria smiled. "He won't say. My guess is it's stashed somewhere on Turgut's property. That's his brother. He told Turgut all about his involvement with the Black Hand and I wouldn't be surprised if they came to some sort of agreement. Habab and Tikrit will go back there tomorrow morning while we transport Ismet to Izmir."

"We're staying in Usak overnight?"

"Yes, unless you have any objections," Sadria said, and quickly added, "I do so hope you will agree."

Bolan looked into her eyes, trying to determine if there was a veiled invitation in the statement. She gave him a friendly smile and not a hint of anything else.

"I could use a cup of coffee. How about you?"

"Sure."

"Good. There's a pot brewing upstairs. Shall we?" Sadria said, and headed out of the cell, issuing instructions to the agents.

The pot turned out to be in a room adjacent to the lieutenant's office, resting on one of four long tables bordered by metal folding chairs.

"This is where they hold meetings," Sadria mentioned while pouring them both steaming cups of Turkish coffee.

Bolan took a sip and glanced out the open door toward the entrance to the police station. He could see the burly officer still working at the counter, and beyond him were two men just entering the building. Oddly they held their chins tucked to their chests, as if they didn't want their faces to be seen, and each had an arm behind his back. The warrior's combat-honed instincts blared a warning in his mind and he started to step toward the doorway.

Both men had stopped, and the taller of the two now straightened, calling out to the burly officer at the same instant he whipped an Uzi from behind his back.

Muzaffer Dora. Bolan recognized the terrorist immediately from the photograph he'd seen; there was no mistaking that facial scar. He went for his Beretta.

Dora's Uzi burped, the 9 mm parabellum manglers catching the officer in the head and propelling him backward even as the second man pitched a square object at the counter. Both terrorists promptly bolted.

The Beretta had almost cleared leather when Bolan realized the significance of the action. He spun and leaped, wrapping his left arm around Sadria's waist, sweeping her toward the floor. She involuntarily cried out and spilled her cup of coffee. As they came down hard between a pair of chairs, the world seemed to be coming to an end. A deafening explosion rocked the entire structure, causing the floor to heave under them, and for a second Bolan thought it would buckle completely. He scrambled forward under a table, hauling Sadria with him, hearing windows shatter and walls topple all around them. A thunderous crash occurred nearby, and something heavy struck the table-top, almost snapping the legs. Dust swirled into the air, forming a choking cloud that obscured everything.

"Mike—" Sadria said, a tinge of terror in her tone.

"Quiet," Bolan ordered, keeping his mouth and nose low to the floor to avoid inhaling the dust.

Loud shouts arose, followed by more gunfire, the quick bursts of automatic weapons. Someone screamed. Someone else cursed.

The warrior lifted his head and looked over his shoulder. He realized they would be dead if the table had been a shade weaker. The wall bordering the hallway had been flattened by the blast, smashing down on the very spot where they'd been standing moments earlier, with several heavy beams lying on top of the table amid smaller broken pieces of wood and mortar.

A man suddenly began to scream in Turkish, repeating the same words over and over.

"That's Ismet Vahdettin," Sadria whispered. "He's begging someone not to shoot him. What's going on?"

"It's the Black Hand," Bolan informed her, crawling backward, seeking a way out of the tangled debris so he could go to Vahdettin's aid.

A single loud shot punctuated the pleading.

The warrior twisted onto his right side. Large sections of the wall and other rubble formed a tangled barrier. There wasn't room to stand although there were gaps here and there large enough to squeeze through. "Stay here," he said, and worked his way over to an opening.

More shots rang out, the crack of pistols mixed with the chatter of submachine guns.

Bolan's lips compressed into a grim line. The officers who survived the explosion were putting up a determined fight, but from the sound of things they were clearly outgunned and the outcome inevitable unless he could help even the odds. His duffel bag was still stashed in the trunk of Sadria's car; he'd have to make do with the Beretta and rely on stealth.

He cleared the first gap and crawled to a second, picking his way carefully to avoid sharp glass fragments, nails and jutting pieces of jagged wood.

Behind him something rustled.

Bolan looked back and saw Sadria following. "I thought I told you to stay put."

"Not on your life. Two of the men who work under me are out there and in trouble. You're not leaving me behind."

"Are you armed?"

Sadria reached under her blazer and pulled out an MKE pistol, a small piece of hardware that packed a hefty 9 mm wallop. "Will this do?" she whispered.

Nodding, Bolan continued in the general direction of the entrance.

Moments later he glimpsed the debris-strewed area where the counter had once stood. Skirting a thick beam, he spied a wide space ahead and beyond it the waiting area. The shooting had stopped, and he knew what he would find once he cleared the barrier.

"Wait for me," Sadria said.

The warrior slowed but continued on his hands and knees until he reached the last opening. With the Beretta clutched firmly in his right hand, he peered out.

Whatever explosive the terrorists had used had done the job well. Whole portions of the ceiling had caved in, all of the walls were cracked and many had fallen. A four-foot-wide hole indicated the exact spot where the detonator went off. A pair of blood-covered legs protruded from under a huge slab that had crushed a hapless officer to a pulp. Not far away lay a severed human arm.

Bolan stepped out cautiously. Glancing to the left he spied the bullet-riddled body of Habab, facedown in a spreading crimson pool. He moved warily toward the stairs, stepping over debris, and stopped at the top.

Halfway down, lying on his back, his face pock-marked with holes, was Tikrit. At the bottom of the stairs, slumped over on his knees with his head turned toward the stairs, sporting a dark cavity in the middle of his forehead, was Ismet Vahdettin.

The Black Hand had been ruthlessly efficient.

Sadria stepped next to the warrior and voiced a horrified exclamation in Turkish. She ran down to Tikrit and knelt, probed for a pulse and closed her eyes in sorrow.

Bolan wheeled and went to the waiting area, searching for officers who might be alive. There were none. He crossed to the entrance. The door had been torn from its hinges by the blast and was lying on the sidewalk. Holding the Beretta in a two-handed grip, he poked his head outside and looked both ways.

People were converging on the police station from all over, shouting to one another. A car was bearing down from the east.

He studied the vehicle and recognized it as a patrol car. It suddenly occurred to him that the officers who had been on patrol wouldn't have any idea who he was; they might open fire first and wonder about his identity later. He pivoted, intending to get Sadria, but there she was standing a yard away, tears moistening the corners of her eyes, her arms limp at her sides, dazed by the slaughter.

"Everyone is dead," she said woodenly. "Every last one of them."

"I know." Bolan moved closer to gently place his right hand on her shoulder. "This might seem cruel, but you've got to get a grip on yourself. There are police coming and dozens of citizens."

Sadria nodded slowly. "I understand." She dabbed at her eyes with her sleeves and cleared her throat, blinking a few times. "I'll be all right. Don't worry."

Bolan holstered the Beretta, wondering if she'd ever been involved in a shootout before. Maybe Arpinar confined her duties to the administrative end of the department. He decided it would be tactless to inquire now.

Replacing her MKE, Sadria went outside just as the patrol screeched to a stop. She produced her ID as the cops leaped out. People were gathering on both sides, conversing animatedly and pointing at the building.

Bolan watched her talk to the officers, who then ran past him into the devastated station.

"They heard the explosion half a mile away, came this way to investigate and saw the crowd gathering," Sadria told him. "I asked them to—"

A gray-haired man in a brown cap stepped forward and interrupted her, excitedly explaining something. He pointed westward along E23.

"He says he was a block from here when it happened," Sadria translated. "He saw two men run out of the building. Both were carrying guns and the taller one was laughing. They jumped into a green car and it sped off to the west. He believes a woman was driving."

"They could be on their way to Izmir," Bolan speculated. Where else would they go? Dora might find a secluded spot to hide somewhere along E23, but he doubted it. The three Black Hand members would be safer in a major city, and they were probably planning to rejoin their comrades, unaware that Nur was dead, Mithat had fled and the hostages had been freed.

Sadria glanced at the highway, then at Bolan. "We might be able to overtake them if we leave immediately and drive like hell."

"There's a chance," Bolan conceded, noting her expectant expression. "I'm game if you are."

"Let's get the bastards," Sadria said. "First let me give instructions to the police." She ran inside.

Bolan moved to their car and discovered the rear window on the passenger side had been broken by a flying piece of debris. He didn't have long to wait before Sadria joined him again, fishing the keys from a pocket.

"I'll do the driving."

"Okay. Unlock the trunk so I can get my duffel."

Sadria complied, and moments later they were roaring down E23.

12

"Did you see the look on Vahdettin's face when I squeezed the trigger?" Dora asked no one in particular.

Nain spoke sarcastically from the back seat. "Yes, I saw it. Terrorizing that old man certainly proved how brave you are."

Dora twisted, hatred flaring briefly in his narrowed eyes. He glanced at the AK-47 in Nain's lap and scowled. "Your insult is uncalled for, brother. I've proved my bravery time and again."

"I don't dispute that. But there was no need for you to play with Vahdettin as you did. Moving your Uzi back and forth in front of his eyes while he begged for his life was unnecessarily cruel. You've changed a lot in the past two years, Muzo."

"Have I?"

Nain nodded and gazed out the window at the scenery streaking past. "In the old days you would have shot him and been done with it. Now you seem to take an excessive delight in tormenting those you terminate."

"I wouldn't describe impressing on him the error of his ways as cruel," Dora stated stiffly. "You tend to exaggerate sometimes."

"Perhaps."

"You're far more discontent than I imagined," Dora commented. "I'm surprised I didn't notice it sooner."

Yeni suddenly spoke up. "There's a turnoff up ahead. Should I take it?" Her hands were clamped tightly on the steering wheel. She looked at the speedometer, which indicated they were doing over eighty, and swallowed nervously.

"Keep going," Dora instructed her.

"But the police—" she began.

"Are lazy fools. Do you see them on our tail?"

A check of the side and rearview mirrors failed to disclose any sign of flashing beacons to their rear. There were a few pairs of headlights, the closest more than a half mile away. "No," Yeni said, relieved.

"And you won't. It's been ten minutes since we left Usak. If they were after us we'd have seen them by now. The cops are too busy pulling their fellow officers from the rubble. By the time they get around to sending a patrol car this way, we'll be almost to Izmir."

"Then can I slow down?" Yeni requested. She took a curve sharply, furiously spinning the wheel, the tires squealing.

"Perhaps you'd better or we'll never reach Izmir alive."

Nain interjected a thought. "The police in Usak are bound to phone other towns and put out an alert. They'll probably notify the authorities in Izmir, too."

"Sooner or later they'll get around to it," Dora agreed. "But we're talking about country cops here. They'll take their good sweet time."

"I'd rather be safe than sorry," Nain said. "We have to go through Salihli and Turgutlu before we reach Izmir. Perhaps it would be wise to bypass both towns. We'll lose a little time, but what is time compared to the possibility of losing our lives?"

Dora looked at him. "I'm not the only one who has changed. You weren't so concerned about dying when we began our campaign."

"I've learned a few things since our college days. One of them is that life is precious and sweet. I look forward to spending my later years in a small house overlooking the Aegean or the Mediterranean."

"You're quite the dreamer. That's part of your problem."

Nain faced forward. "I wasn't aware I had a problem."

"Just a figure of speech. I just meant that out of all of us, you have the greatest imagination. You envision things we would never dream of."

They continued for a while in silence.

"I just hope I can make it safely out of the country to Europe before all hell breaks loose," Nain remarked. "The government undoubtedly will intensify its efforts to apprehend us after tonight."

"So?" Dora said contemptuously. "They haven't caught us yet, and they never will. We always manage to stay one step ahead of the incompetent fools."

"Everyone's luck runs out sooner or later."

"Is that a fact? You're beginning to depress me with your dismal attitude. Unless you have something constructive to say, do me a favor and keep quiet until we get to Izmir."

"I'll talk when I damn well feel like it," Nain snarled, placing his right hand on the AK-47. "You're not our lord and master, despite what you apparently think."

"I never claimed to be," Dora stated. "But I have managed to keep all of us from rotting in prison, haven't I?"

Nain's features had hardened. "You make it sound as if you do all the planning and the work," he told Dora. "We contribute to the cause just as much as you do. For the past ten or eleven months, though, you've been treating us as if we're your flunkies. You see yourself as better than we are."

"Now we're getting to the heart of the matter," Dora said. "None of what you say is true. But you've convinced yourself that I'm some sort of tyrant. The real reason you want out is because you're fed up with me. Why don't you admit it?"

"I've already given you my reasons."

Dora smirked. "What's the matter? Are you afraid to tell the truth?"

"Save your petty arguments for later," Yeni snapped. "We have a bigger problem at the moment."

"What are you talking about?" Dora demanded.

"I think someone is after us."

Dora and Nain shifted so they could stare out the rear window. A quarter of a mile distant were headlights, closing rapidly.

"It can't be the police," Nain said. "There are no lights on top and I don't hear sirens."

"I've been watching them for several minutes," Yeni disclosed. "Whoever they are, they haven't let up on the gas once."

"Pick up speed," Dora directed. "Let's see if we can lose them."

"And if we can't?" Yeni asked, bringing the speedometer back to eighty.

"We can't afford to take any chances." Dora nodded at the rear window. "Why don't you roll that down, Ahmet, and prepare a suitable reception? If they catch us, empty your magazine into their vehicle."

"And if it's just some guy who likes to drive fast?"

"He picked the wrong night to take a drive."

"THERE'S ANOTHER ONE up ahead."

"I see it," Bolan replied as their car shot out of a tight curve and hit a straightaway. He had his right hand on the dash for support, his left resting on the Uzi nestled in his lap. So far they'd passed two cars and a battered pickup. Neither of the cars had been green.

"If this isn't the one, do we keep going?" Sadria asked. "I don't see any other taillights up ahead, and we haven't seen any sign of them. Based on your experience, is it worth our while to continue?"

"I don't believe in quitting with a job half finished."

Sadria nodded. "Then we keep going even if this one isn't them."

Their sedan gradually narrowed the gap. Frequently they would lose sight of the other vehicle when it went around a curve, its lights temporarily screened by the roadside vegetation.

"Whoever it is, they're really moving," Sadria remarked.

Bolan tried to distinguish the vehicle's color but couldn't. There were few streetlights this far out in the country.

"If it is them, how will you stop their car? Shoot out the tires?"

Bolan looked at her. "The tires?"

"Yes. We must try to take them alive, after all."

"You want them alive after what they did in Usak?"

"I believe in going by the letter of the law, remember?" Sadria reminded him, her gaze glued to the highway. "Yes, I want to get them for what they did back there, but I want to take them into custody if at all possible and see that they stand trial for their heinous crimes."

The big man shook his head. "Never happen. We're not dealing with common criminals here. The Black Hand won't let themselves be taken alive."

"You don't know that for certain."

"Yeah, I do."

"Are you suggesting we don't even try?"

Bolan remained silent.

"I knew it," Sadria stated testily.

The Executioner looked out the side window, concealing his annoyance. This situation, he mentally noted, was a prime example of why he preferred to work alone. People like Sadria, those who saw the world in varying shades of gray instead of the realistic hues of black and white, were too compassionate. They couldn't seem to comprehend the true nature of evil or recognize the varied guises of Animal Man. They failed to understand that hard-core killers such as Muzaffer Dora enjoyed pulling the trigger. The Doras of the world were the human equivalent of rabid dogs, mad at everyone and everything and perfectly willing to blow away complete innocents without any provocation whatsoever.

Their car took yet another turn, and now the vehicle they were chasing was only a few hundred yards off.

"It seems to be slowing," Sadria commented.

The warrior looked, and sure enough the vehicle had reduced speed. Why? One minute it was going like a bat out of hell, the next at the speed limit. He worked the cocking handle on the Uzi.

"I trust you won't open fire until we establish whether it is the Black Hand."

"Sarcasm, Ms. Inonu, doesn't become you," Bolan said, as he focused his attention on the vehicle.

She glanced at him, then concentrated on overtaking the car up head. "Sorry. I didn't mean to be insulting."

"Yeah, you did."

"It's slowing even more," Sadria declared after a moment of silence.

The car they were pursuing had reduced speed to between forty and fifty miles per hour. It hugged the shoulder, as if the driver were giving them plenty of room to pass.

"I don't like this," Bolan told her. "Slow down."

Sadria followed his advice and cut back to the speed limit.

"Go just a little faster than it's going until we're about five car-lengths back, then match its speed," Bolan told her. "Approach from the rear. If it's them and you pull alongside, they'll cut loose out the windows."

"I'm suddenly very nervous," Sadria said, doing as he instructed.

"It's only natural. But you'll do all right if worse comes to worst."

"How can you be so sure?"

"I saw how well you handled yourself at the police station."

Their headlights finally struck the car ahead.

"It's green!" Sadria exclaimed.

Bolan nodded grimly. "Take it nice and slow. Let's see how many people are inside."

Anxious seconds elapsed as they crept nearer.

"I only see one," Sadria stated. "There's a woman doing the driving."

"Just like the guy in Usak told us."

"But where are the two men?"

"They might have switched to another vehicle or they could be crouched on the floor. We'll know soon."

For over a minute the two vehicles cruised westward. The woman never indicated in any way that she knew they were there.

"Shouldn't I try to pull her over?" Sadria asked.

"No. We let them make the first move."

"And if by some fluke it isn't the Black Hand?"

Bolan saw the woman glance over her right shoulder at them. "Quick. Drop farther back."

But before Sadria could comply a man rose up in the green car's back seat, leaned out the open rear window on the driver's side and trained an AK-47 on their windshield.

13

Sadria reacted superbly, spinning the wheel to the right and angling toward the shoulder even as she applied the brakes.

The terrorist opened fire, snapping off a hasty burst and missing. He twisted, attempting to track them, and almost lost his grip on the AK-47 when the green car swung abruptly into a sharp curve.

Bolan rolled down his window as Sadria accelerated, easing out until his stomach rested on the top of the door. Leveling the Uzi, he braced his legs against the front seat as they took the curve. A moment later they were in the clear and racing down a short straightaway, and there was the Black Hand's vehicle ten car-length's in front, the gunner now inside and staring out the back window.

"Hang on," Sadria shouted, flooring the accelerator.

The warrior elevated the Uzi to compensate for the range and squeezed off a dozen rounds.

Sparks danced off the green car's trunk, and the rear window shattered and dissolved into cubes of glass. Instantly the car went into a series of wide swerves as the driver frantically tried to evade further rounds.

Bolan tried to fix a reliable bead on the elusive target. A curve materialized, nipping his intent in the bud, compelling him to wait until they were out of it and rocketing in pursuit. Yet another curve unexpectedly appeared, thwarting him again.

Mountainous terrain hemmed in the highway. The engineers had followed the path of least resistance, snaking the ribbon of asphalt through a virtual maze of peaks and hills. The stretch ahead twisted right and left continuously, the worst stretch between Izmir and Usak.

Her knuckles white from the intense pressure of her hands on the steering wheel, her body rigid from nervous tension, Sadria was doing her best to catch the green car. She whipped the wheel deftly, taking the bends tight and fast, gaining yardage bit by bit.

Bolan slid onto the seat, knowing it would be futile to try to cripple the other vehicle until they were on the plain below the mountains. He hadn't seen the woman's features clearly, but simple deduction told him Yeni Yurukoglu was doing the driving for the opposition. The guy who had tried to take them out with the AK-47 hadn't been Muzaffer Dora, so it had to have been Ahmet Nain.

"Ten more miles and we'll be out of these damn mountains," Sadria mentioned, her face the epitome of determination. "We'll get them then."

"You're doing great," Bolan told her, and meant it. "You can ease off the gas a bit. Trying to get close on these curves would be suicide. Just stay on their tail until we hit the flatland."

With evident reluctance Sadria did as instructed. "Luck is on our side. As best I can remember there are no turnoffs until Salihli, which is thirty or forty miles from here. The terrorists are stuck on E23.''

Bolan watched the green car's taillights swing into a wide curve. "They'll make their move long before we reach Salihli. Stay alert."

She nodded and worked the wheel, her right foot shifting smoothly from the gas to the brake and back again. "I must say that I find fieldwork very invigorating. I think I'll ask for more of it."

"Tired of a desk job?"

"Tired of being a glorified messenger. Mehmet sends me to all the conferences and meetings he doesn't want to attend. Every now and then he's let me take part in an interrogation. But he's never allowed me to participate in making an arrest."

Bolan braced his right hand on the dash to keep from swaying to the right or left every time they rounded a bend, his eyes riveted to the red lights ahead, alert for any sudden slowing or other deviation.

"I suppose you're accustomed to this sort of thing."

"I've been in my fair share of hot spots," Bolan conceded.

"Are you ever afraid?"

"No. Not in the sense you mean."

"Aren't you afraid of dying?"

"I don't dwell on death. I just do what needs to be done."

The green car suddenly spurted ahead, tearing into a curve while doing thirty miles over the speed limit.

"What are they trying to pull?" Sadria mused aloud, accelerating. "They must know they can't lose us on this road."

"Be careful."

Dense woodland bordered the highway on both sides, and for several seconds the taillights were obscured by the trees.

The curve wound to the right. Sadria hugged the center line, her arms locked to keep the steering wheel steady, her body inclined toward the warrior. Her foot stayed on the gas pedal, the tires shrieking in protest.

Bolan kept his eyes on E23. There were no other vehicles anywhere in sight, not even when they rounded the curve, and he tensed in consternation at finding the taillights gone. Almost instantly he detected an incongruous shape among the trees on his side of the road. "Ambush!" he shouted, and reached out to yank Sadria down beside him on the seat.

"What are you—" she started to protest, her left hand still gripping the wheel.

And then the AK-47 and two other automatic weapons unleashed a withering barrage of lead, the rounds hitting home with jackhammer rapidity.

The windshield and the other windows were reduced to bits and pieces in the blink of an eye, spraying over the occupants of the front seat. Bolan covered his eyes with his right hand as glass struck his head and shoulders. Some of the slugs penetrated the doors and drilled into the seat, the floor and the dash. Something stung his right calf. A slight pain seared his right shoulder. He heard both tires on his side of the vehicle blow, and the car went into a skid.

"We'll crash!" Sadria shouted, starting to rise.

"Stay down," Bolan commanded, pulling on her arm.

Suddenly Sadria arched her back and clutched at her temple, gasping in agony, then pitched forward.

The warrior twisted and managed to catch her, but no sooner were his arms looped around her shoulders than their car swung sideways and the tires on the driver's side left the ground. For a sickening moment it seemed the vehicle would go all the way over, but the tires bounced down again with a brutal impact.

Bolan held on tight to Sadria and glanced up in time to see several inky trees looming high above them. He pulled his legs onto the seat and braced for the tremendous crash that occurred a heartbeat later.

The collision tossed the Executioner and the woman about as if they were weightless. Bolan hurtled toward the driver's door, Sadria still clutched in his arms, and smashed into the steering wheel, bruising his right side. The breath whooshed out of him as he was thrown back again, somehow becoming upended in the process.

Suddenly all motion ceased and an oppressive silence enveloped the car. The big man's ears were ringing and his ribs ached. Grunting, he got to his knees on the seat and found Sadria beside him, the lower half of her body lying on the floor. By some miracle he still had the Uzi in his right hand.

Although Bolan wanted to check on his companion, he had a more urgent priority. He heard an engine being gunned and glanced out the broken rear window to see the terrorists' vehicle backing onto E23. Sliding over Sadria, he grabbed the door handle and shoved.

The green car began to accelerate.

Bolan leveled the Uzi the instant his feet touched the grass even though the car was already almost to the next curve. His finger began to tighten on the trigger, but he held his fire rather than waste ammo. He lowered the Uzi in frustration, watched the car disappear and turned.

The dim glow of the overhead light showed that Sadria was still unconscious, her left cheek resting in a crimson puddle.

The warrior placed the Uzi on the roof and slid in, discovering the passenger side had been partially crumpled by the crash. The opposite door had buckled and the front end resembled an accordion.

Bolan leaned down and gently brushed Sadria's hair aside to expose the wound. He expelled a breath of relief at finding only a deep crease several inches long on her right temple, the blood flow reduced to a mere trickle. Sliding his hands under her arms, he slowly pulled her onto the seat, backing out as he did, until she was lying flat on her back and he stood just outside the car.

Sadria groaned and her eyelids fluttered.

The Executioner pivoted and looked both ways along the highway, which was forty feet off. The Black Hand had disappeared around another curve to the west, and there were no other vehicles in sight. Since Sadria would require stitches, his first priority was to get her to a doctor. Hitching a ride was their best option. He retrieved his duffel from the back seat, deposited the Uzi inside and slung the heavy canvas bag over his left shoulder. Next he gingerly eased Sadria from the car and cradled her in his arms. Her head slumped against his chest and she groaned again.

Squaring his shoulders, Bolan hiked toward the road. He stared out over the mountainous expanse surrounding them, fully realizing how isolated they were. Given the speed they'd maintained, he estimated they were about halfway between Usak and Salihli. If worse came to worst and he had to walk, he decided it would be wiser to head for Salihli. At least the going would be primarily downhill until he hit the plain.

"Mike—?"

The softly spoken inquiry brought Bolan to a halt. He looked down and found Sadria's eyes open and fixed on his face. "Don't talk. Rest until I get us out of here."

"My head hurts like hell."

"You have a flesh wound. It's not serious, but we should get you to a doctor."

"Let me walk."

"No way. Just take it easy."

"I insist," Sadria persisted. "Set me down. I'll be all right."

Against his better judgment Bolan slowly lowered her feet to the ground.

"Thank you," Sadria said, reaching up to touch her temple. She took a step backward. "See? I'm fine."

Bolan knew better and simply waited.

"Did we crash?"

"Yes. We can forget about the car."

Sadria frowned and went to turn. Her legs abruptly gave out and she crumpled.

In a quick motion Bolan scooped her up. She moaned, her chin drooping, and feebly tried to move her arms. "See my point?" he asked.

"Yes."

"Good. Even flesh wounds aren't to be taken lightly, especially to the head." Bolan hefted her lightly and walked toward E23. "Plus we were battered around pretty badly in the collision. Does anything else other than your head hurt?"

"No."

"We won't take any chances. You'll walk when I say you can."

Sadria's right hand came up and gently touched his cheek. "Whatever you say."

Bolan became acutely conscious of the heat of her body and the feel of her left breast on his shirt. He shook his head and concentrated on the critical matter at hand.

"What happened to the Black Hand?" Sadria inquired.

"They took off," Bolan answered, gazing to the west as he came to the shoulder of the road, glad it was too dark for her to note the concern in his eyes.

"Traffic is light at this time of night," Sadria mentioned. "And this isn't America. Few motorists will stop to pick up strangers in such a remote area."

"Keep quiet and rest. Let me worry about finding transportation."

Sadria ignored him. "Your best bet is to head for Salihli," she suggested.

"I'm planning to. Now be quiet."

The sound of a car engine arose to the east, approaching rapidly.

"Maybe we'll get out of here sooner than we figured," Bolan noted, stepping to the edge of the highway. He put what he hoped to be a friendly smile on his face and pivoted in the direction of the oncoming vehicle.

"You might convince them to stop if you call out to them," Sadria said. "The Turkish word for help is *imdat.*"

Moments later a brown station wagon that had been in its prime more than a decade earlier zoomed around the curve and shot toward them.

Bolan waved his right hand as the headlight beams played over them. *"Imdat!"* he shouted. *"Imdat!"*

The station wagon slowed abruptly, but only for several seconds, long enough for the driver to get a good look at them. But instead of braking, the man at the wheel swerved to the left and stepped on the gas, roaring past them into the night.

"Damn," Bolan muttered, watching in annoyance as the station wagon vanished around the next bend.

"I told you," Sadria noted softly. "Occasionally there are robbers in these parts. Getting someone to stop will not be easy."

"Then we do it the hard way," Bolan said, resigning himself to the long hike ahead. He didn't bother to bring up the possibility lurking in the back of his mind. Why bother worrying her even more? Striding briskly, his shoes crunching on the thin strip of gravel bordering the road, he mentally crossed his fingers and hoped for the best.

14

Muzaffer Dora suddenly slapped his thigh in anger and glanced at Yeni Yurukoglu. "Turn around."

She stared at him. "What?"

"Are you hard-of-hearing?" Dora snapped. "Turn the car around and head back."

Ahmet Nain leaned forward from the back seat and asked, "Why do you want to go back there?"

"Because we're fools."

"In what way?" Nain inquired.

"We were in such a hurry to get away that we didn't make certain the bastards were dead."

Nain shrugged. "What difference does it make if the cops survived? Returning is too risky."

"I don't give a damn about the risk," Dora said, glaring at his fellow terrorist. "It just occurred to me that the people in that car weren't police officers. They had to be with Arpinar's department."

"You don't know that," Nain said skeptically.

"Don't I?" Dora countered. "Where were the flashing lights on their car? Where was the siren? That wasn't a police cruiser."

"It could have been an unmarked car," Yeni spoke up.

Dora directed his anger at her. "Don't be stupid. Unmarked cars are only found in the larger cities. The police force in Usak is small. All they have are marked patrol vehicles."

"You don't know that for certain," Nain noted. "You're just guessing."

"And it's a good guess," Dora countered. "But since you doubt my logic and seem to want proof, didn't you notice the weapon they used?"

"A submachine gun of some kind," Nain said.

"It was an Uzi. I'd bet my life on it." Dora paused and smugly regarded his companions. "Since when do police officers stationed in small towns use Uzis?"

"Never," Yeni admitted.

"But Arpinar's fascist bloodhounds are known to sometimes carry such hardware," Dora pointed out. "Between their car and the Uzi there is no question that those were the illustrious director's men. They must have been elsewhere when we attacked the station."

"You're right," Yeni agreed. "As usual."

"Then why haven't you turned around yet?" Dora demanded in annoyance.

Obediently Yeni trod on the brakes, brought the car to a screeching halt and executed a tight U-turn. In moments they were racing eastward along E23, a cool breeze blowing through their missing rear window.

"I don't like this," Nain said.

Dora snorted in disgust. "Yeni is right. You've become too squeamish for your own good." He frowned. "For *our* own good."

"We've always prided ourselves on being extremely careful at all times," Nain observed. "We've lasted so long because we never leave anything to chance. And yet here we are, committing a reckless blunder because you can't control your hatred of Mehmet Arpinar and the government.''

''A little recklessness is the price one must pay to indulge in sweet revenge,'' Dora said.

''Wait until Orhan and Nur hear about this.''

''They will agree I was right,'' Dora predicted. ''They hate the government's counterterrorist agents as much as I do, Orhan possibly more.''

His displeasure etched on his face, Nain sat back and shook his head.

''How do you want me to do this?'' Yeni inquired. ''Should I just drive past their car so we can have a look, or should I pull right up to it?''

''Once we're a few hundred yards from where we ambushed them, go slow,'' Dora instructed her. ''We don't know exactly how many were in that car, and some might still be alive.'' He shifted and glanced over his shoulder. ''And you, my dear Ahmet, can make yourself useful by getting a few grenades out of that box on the floor. If it's not too much trouble.''

''It's no trouble,'' Nain said sullenly.

''Thank you,'' Dora said, his tone tinged with scorn. ''And cheer up. This shouldn't take long. In thirty minutes the government dogs will be dead and we'll be on our way to Izmir.''

BOLAN HAD WALKED for only five minutes before he spotted the low structure off to the left, forty yards from E23. He halted. The walls were pale in the moonlight and the roof seemed to sag in the center.

There were no lights on, no evidence whatsoever of its being occupied.

Sadria stirred in his arms and looked up. "Why have you stopped?"

"There's a building over there," Bolan informed her, nodding.

Twisting, Sadria studied it for a bit. "An abandoned house would be my guess. Many rural people have given up on the hard country life and moved to the already-overcrowded cities."

"We'll rest there awhile," Bolan proposed, and headed across the highway.

"There's no need," Sadria objected. "I'm feeling much better. My head doesn't ache quite as badly. Put me down and I'll show you I can hold my own."

"Don't start that again."

Sadria sighed in frustration. "Has anyone ever told you that you can be quite hardheaded?"

"Only those who know me best."

Her teeth flashed as she grinned. "You are always honest and direct. I admire such traits in a man."

Bolan left the road and entered a weed-choked field. A few partially rotted wooden posts indicated where a fence had once stood. There were several isolated trees between E23 and the house. Off to the right and the left were relatively barren hills.

Up close the house turned out to be in terrible condition. The middle of the roof might well come crashing down at the next heavy rain, and other sections were missing, torn off by high winds. The left wall slanted outward at a precarious angle. There were countless cracks everywhere, no glass in any of the windows, and the door hung on one hinge, tilted inward.

Exercising caution, Bolan stepped to the threshold and peered inside. A musty scent tingled his nostrils. Any furniture had long since been removed. Cobwebs hung in the corners of the ceiling. Several large bird feathers lay under a window, bathed in a dim glow.

"This place has all the comforts," Sadria quipped.

"I'm going to set you down," Bolan warned her. "Don't make any sudden moves or you might become dizzy."

The warrior eased her to the floor just inside the door, then moved into the room and looked up at the cracked ceiling. The four main support beams were still intact, and he concluded the roof wouldn't fall on them.

"We could start a fire," Sadria suggested.

"In a bit," Bolan said, listening to the faint sound of a car on the highway. He stepped to a window and gazed out to see a vehicle traveling rapidly from west to east. The distance prevented him from distinguishing the color.

Sadria strolled over to him. "Perhaps we should spend the night here."

"We have to get your wound taken care of," Bolan said, his eyes on the car until it disappeared.

"My head is much better. The bleeding has stopped, and the pain is almost gone. I'll be all right until morning. Besides, during the day the traffic on E23 is much heavier and we should be able to get a lift without any problem."

"We'll rest here for a while and then we'll see."

Sadria placed her hands on her hips. "Who are you trying to kid? You don't need a rest. You're doing this for me, right?"

"Partly," Bolan admitted, and propped his hands on the windowsill. He liked the setup. The pasture gave him a clear field of fire should his hunch prove correct. If not, her idea had a definite appeal.

"Something is bothering you. What is it?" Sadria inquired, examining his profile.

"Nothing."

"You don't lie very well."

Bolan glanced at her. "Why don't *you* find a spot to lie down? I'll collect some wood shortly and build a small fire."

"I'm not tired."

"Do it anyway."

Displaying obvious reluctance, Sadria moved to the left side of the room and sat down. "What did you do before you took up your current line of work?" she inquired.

"A little of this, a little of that."

"I would wager a year's pay that you were in the military. You have a soldier's air about you."

"You think so?" Bolan asked absently, gazing eastward, wondering how long it would be before he found out if his caution was warranted. The odds were fifty-fifty. By all rights the terrorists should never have left the scene without first verifying the hits, and he fully expected them to realize their amateurish mistake and return.

"I know so," Sadria stated. "You give orders as naturally as some people breathe. I bet you were an officer."

"You'd lose your money," Bolan said, tensing when a pair of headlights appeared to the east. If the car he'd seen a minute ago was the Black Hand's, this could be them coming back. But it quickly sped out of sight, going way too fast to be the terrorists.

"If we're going to be stuck here all night, the least you could do is be more talkative. I'm only trying to be friendly."

The reproach made Bolan turn sideways so he could keep an eye on the highway and her. "What do you want to talk about?"

"You."

"Pick another subject."

"Why? Don't you like discussing yourself? Wait. I think I understand. You don't want anyone prying into your personal life, is that it?"

"My past is my own business," Bolan admitted frankly. "In my line of work, as you put it, it's not wise to let other people know personal details that could later be used against me."

"Such as?"

"Information concerning family or friends. People have tried to get to me that way."

"So you're afraid you'll slip and tell me something I shouldn't know? Even if you did, who would I tell?"

"I don't—" Bolan began, and stopped when he saw another car coming from the east, this one moving much slower than the last. He watched intently and saw it slow a bit when it was directly abreast of the abandoned house. Almost immediately the driver accelerated, and the car went around the next curve to the west.

"Why are you spending so much time at that window?" Sadria inquired. "What is so interesting out there?"

The warrior said nothing. He unslung the duffel bag and deposited it at his feet. Leaning down, he unfastened the hook and reached in.

"What are you doing?" Sadria asked.

"Playing it safe," Bolan answered, pulling out the Uzi. He heard her rise and step over to his side.

"It's the Black Hand, isn't it? They've returned to finish us off."

"There's a possibility they might." Bolan removed the magazine and rummaged in the duffel for a fresh one.

Sadria gazed out the window at the field. "Why didn't you warn me sooner?"

"Because I didn't want to alarm you for no reason. It's not certain they'll come back for us."

"I don't like being patronized."

"Chew me out later," Bolan suggested, his fingers closing on the magazine. He slapped it in, worked the cocking handle and held out the submachine gun. "Do you know how to use one of these?"

"I've shot Uzis on the firing range."

"Take it."

"What will you use?" Sadria asked, complying.

"I have a few other goodies in here," Bolan said. He took out the Desert Eagle and secured the pistol in his belt. Next he removed his partially fieldstripped M-16. Since the flash suppressor and upper barrel would have jutted out of the duffel, he'd separated the upper receiver group from the lower receiver group, essentially dividing the weapon in two, and stashed the shorter pieces side by side.

"I don't suppose you have a tank in there."

"Sorry. My tank was in the shop for repairs," Bolan responded. He placed the two halves of the M-16 together and reseated the receiver pivot pin.

"Are you about done?"

"Almost. Why?"

"Because someone is coming to pay us a visit," Sadria said, nodding toward the window.

The warrior looked and spied an indistinct form moving toward the house from the highway.

15

Ahmet Nain was fit to be tied.

Years earlier, when the Black Hand initially organized, he'd deeply respected Muzaffer Dora and regarded the leader of their small revolutionary cell as the perfect terrorist, as wise, witty and supremely devoted to the cause. Now, after having worked as a glorified lackey for more months than he cared to remember, he knew otherwise.

Somewhere along the line his friend had changed drastically, becoming dictatorial and paranoid. Instead of regarding the other members as equals, he began viewing them as inferiors whose sole purpose in life was to obey his every command. The autocratic tendencies had increased to the point where the others, with the possible exception of Orhan, were reluctant to voice dissenting opinions for fear of arousing Muzo's anger.

The man had become unbearable. It was Muzo's erratic behavior, more than anything else, that made Ahmet want out of the Black Hand, a reason he didn't dare confess. He simply couldn't take it anymore. He refused to be treated so shabbily by someone whose ego would fill a football stadium.

After tonight, Ahmet told himself, it would all be over. Once they were in Izmir he'd pack and head for the border. Within twenty-four hours he would be safely in Europe where neither Muzo nor the government would ever find him. All he had to do was get through the night.

Was that all?

The thought prompted a grin, and he quickly caught himself and concentrated on the matter at hand. As if it weren't bad enough that Muzo had insisted on going to Usak to hunt down Vahdettin; as if it weren't bad enough that Muzo insisted on attacking the Usak police station; and as if it weren't bad enough that Muzo then decided they should drive back to verify the government agents in the car were dead, the bastard now wanted that dilapidated old house up ahead checked out in case the agents had sought shelter there.

Ahmet scowled and hefted his AK-47. The very idea was crazy, but he had no intention of provoking Muzo when in a few short hours he would be on the road to a new life in Europe. He'd reluctantly agreed to go see, knowing damn well it was a waste of his time, and he angrily recalled Muzo's smug expression as he climbed from the car.

The rotten son of a bitch.

Preoccupied with his dislike of Muzo, Nain almost missed the flicker of movement at one of the windows. Shocked, he instinctively sank to his knees in the weeds. Could it be? The agents hadn't been in the wrecked car, but he'd assumed they'd headed back toward Usak. What if he was wrong and Muzo was right? He flattened and crawled to the right, intending to swing wide around the house and approach it from the rear.

Nain covered fifteen yards and drew up short when the ground sloped sharply downward. He'd stumbled on a narrow gully about three feet deep, running north and south, the ideal cover. Twisting, he went down feetfirst and crouched.

Keeping his head below the rim, peeking out occasionally to mark his progress, Nain crept southward. He estimated the gully passed within fifty feet of the house and grinned. The agents were in for a big surprise.

SEATED IN THE CAR parked just around the next curve to the west, Dora checked his watch and noted that five minutes had elapsed since Ahmet's departure. "I think I should go help him," he commented casually.

Yeni, who had her forearms draped on top of the steering wheel and her forehead resting on her arms, sat up. "Why?"

"Ahmet shouldn't have to do all the dirty work," Dora said, lifting his Uzi.

"He'll be back soon. Why bother?" Yeni asked. She studied his face, anxiety lining her own.

"What a stupid question," Dora said, reaching for the door handle.

"Is it?"

Dora paused, noticed her expression and reined in a surge of anger. Under no circumstances could he let her suspect his motive or she'd be certain to inform the others. "What do you mean?" he inquired.

"I'm worried about Ahmet."

"So am I. That's why I'm going to help him."

"Is that the only reason?" Yeni asked.

Although Dora perceived the implication, he played stupid. "I don't know what you're talking about. What other reason would there be?"

Yeni tapped her fingers on the steering wheel. "Please don't play games with me. I saw the look in your eyes when Ahmet broached the subject of leaving. You were furious."

"So? Isn't my reaction understandable considering how close-knit we've become? We're like a family, aren't we? And I've devoted so much time and energy to our cause, I hate to see our efficiency affected by Ahmet's sudden change of heart."

"We have all made great sacrifices."

"Then what's your point?" Dora asked. He could tell she was in turmoil, fearful of bringing up the heart of the matter, and he smiled to encourage her. It would be better to get everything out in the open now than have to deal with her recriminations later.

"All right. Since you insist on the truth, here it is," Yeni declared. "I'm worried you might harm him."

Laughing as if the idea were ridiculous, Dora let go of the handle. "Why would I want to hurt Ahmet?"

"I know you. I know the way you think. You would never allow one of us to simply pack up and leave the Black Hand. Somehow, someway, you'll stop Ahmet."

Adopting a hurt look, Dora said, "You misjudge me, dear Yeni. Yes, I'll freely admit I would do practically anything to prevent Ahmet from making the biggest mistake of his life. But I would never go so far as to harm him, not after all we have been through." He detected the doubt in her eyes and almost laughed at her gullibility. Then he played his trump card. "If it will make you feel any better, I'll stay here. You can go help Ahmet yourself."

Yeni shook her head. "No, you go ahead," she stated, her guilt transparent. "I'm sorry I made such an accusation. I don't know how I could think you would harm him." She shrugged. "Maybe it's all the stress we've been under lately what with the attack on the American Embassy and kidnapping those tourists."

"I know," Dora said gently as he opened his door. "If a police car should come by, get out of here. Don't wait for us."

"I'll never desert you."

Her loyalty touched him. Dora reached out and gave her arm an affectionate squeeze. "I know I can count on you. You've proved your dedication each time you went to bed with that ass, Pamir. If not for your sacrifice, we wouldn't have obtained the funds we needed to obtain our weapons and other equipment."

"Please, don't remind me of him. When I think of his hands on my body I get goose bumps."

"I envy him."

Yeni glanced at him in surprise. "You do? But you've never displayed any interest in me."

"People change," Dora said with all the false sincerity he could muster. He slid his right leg out the door, pleased at the bewilderment on her face. "We'll talk more later, Yeni. I must go help Ahmet."

"Certainly."

Delighted at the success of his psychological ploy, Dora exited the car, shut the door quietly and jogged eastward along the edge of the road. She would never suspect the truth now. Or if she did, there would be sufficient doubt in her mind to prevent her from mentioning it to anyone else.

How easily most people were manipulated, Dora reflected. With a few rare exceptions the majority of humankind were sheep just waiting to be sheared. The ever-obedient masses blindly conformed to the laws imposed on them by the wealthy elite, seldom questioning the status quo. They could easily be led to the slaughter by men of power and vision.

Dora knew he was such a man. His vision of a Communist Turkey had sustained him for years, and he would manipulate anyone, kill anyone, who stood in the way of having his vision become a reality.

Such as someone who wanted to quit the Black Hand and set a bad example for the others. Such as someone who ran an increased risk of being apprehended in Europe but was too stupid to realize the fact. Ahmet Nain.

THE EXECUTIONER STEPPED back from the window and adjusted the magnification on the night sight of his M-16.

"He's getting closer."

Glancing up, Bolan experienced a twinge of annoyance at seeing her leaning on the windowsill, thoughtlessly exposing herself to the approaching terrorist. He grabbed her arm and pulled her from sight. "Stay away from there."

Surprised, Sadria looked at him, then out at the field. "Oh. Sorry. I wasn't thinking."

Bolan crouched and moved close to the window again. He didn't see the terrorist. Resting the barrel on the sill, he pressed his right eye to the eyepiece and slowly swiveled the rifle back and forth.

The terrorist had gone to ground.

Realizing the implications, Bolan moved back a yard before standing. Whomever was out there—whether Dora, Nain or Yurukoglu—had to know they were in the house. The prospect of being a sitting duck didn't appeal to him, so he quickly hefted the duffel bag over his left shoulder and stepped toward the rear. "Come on."

"Did they see me?"

"Don't know," Bolan said, sparing her feelings. "But we're not taking any chances."

Two small rooms were connected to the living room. One might have served as a bedroom; the other had obviously been the kitchen because an ancient rusted iron stove stood in one corner. At the opposite end was a closed screen door, the lower half ripped to ribbons.

Bolan crossed the kitchen, moved to the left of the screen door and carefully surveyed the land beyond. There were more trees out back than in the front and denser brush, providing plenty of cover. He opened the door slowly, frowning when the hinges squeaked. "We're going to make a run for those trees," he informed Sadria. "Stay close."

Bending at the waist, forced to support the duffel with his left arm and hold the rifle in his right, Bolan darted outside, angling to the southeast, running a zigzag pattern in case one of the terrorists was trying to get a bead on them. He heard Sadria's footsteps and heavy breathing behind him. Together they covered thirty feet and sought shelter behind a tangled thicket.

Except for the sighing breeze, a heavy silence shrouded the countryside. Nothing moved in any direction.

Bolan had a decision to make. Should they stay put or keep going? He wanted to try to nail the terrorists, but remaining entailed a certain risk for Sadria. She was a novice at this sort of thing, and he didn't want her death on his hands. He decided to compromise, to get her away from the house and then return. Rotating, he was about to head southward when she tapped him on the shoulder.

"Where are you going?" Sadria whispered.

"To get you to a safe spot."

"Nonsense. You're being condescending again."

Arguing would prove fruitless and be downright stupid given the circumstances. Reluctantly Bolan put his lips next to her ear and said, "Then you stay right here while I make a sweep of the area. Lie down and don't move no matter what."

Sadria nodded and flattened at the base of the thicket.

The warrior stared at her for a moment, then rose. Staying doubled over he zigzagged to the west, pausing in the shelter of trees and high brush to scour the vicinity of the house for the terrorist.

Bolan traveled twenty yards and crouched next to a stunted tree. Another scan with the scope failed to reveal his enemy. Puzzled, he tried to reason it out. Whomever it was couldn't be trying to sneak close to the house or he'd have spotted him by now. Maybe the one he'd seen, or all three of them, were now positioned at various vantage points and waiting for a clear shot. There was always the possibility the terrorists possessed night-vision devices, and the Executioner's survival instinct dictated he assume they did until proved otherwise.

Again the warrior searched the ground to the west of the house, the logical approach route for the killer he'd spotted, and this time he noticed an irregularity in the terrain, a seemingly shallow depression about fifty feet from the building. But was it shallow, or deep enough to conceal a man? And how far south did it extend?

Bolan dropped onto his stomach and crawled due west to find out. Using his knees and elbows, he snaked along until he abruptly found himself on the eroded rim of a gully. He slipped over the side and lay flat on the bottom, facing toward the highway, and tried to detect movement.

Nothing.

Rising slowly to his knees, Bolan glanced at the house and suddenly realized someone was coming toward him from the direction of the thicket. One look showed him it was Sadria, moving in a crouch. Even as he laid eyes on her he heard a metallic click from somewhere farther along the gully, and the night suddenly spit flame and death.

16

Bolan saw the ground around Sadria erupt in a ragged line of spraying dirt as she frantically threw herself to the left. Pivoting, he spied the muzzle-flash of the terrorist's weapon, which his years of combat experience told him must be an AK-47.

He snapped the M-16 to his shoulder, looked through the night scope and found his target, a man thirty-five feet away. The ghostly image, typical of light amplification devices, had distorted features because the brightness control on the image tube needed to be fine-tuned, but there was no time for such a luxury.

The killer had his elbow propped on the rim of the gully to support the AK-47 and was still firing.

Bolan sighted on the guy's chest and squeezed off three rounds. The high-velocity impact of the 5.56 mm slugs spun the terrorist, then threw him to the ground. He could see only the guy's shoes and lower legs.

Concerned for Sadria, the warrior took his eyes from the terrorist for the few seconds it took to glance at her and see her lying immobile between two bushes. He returned his attention to the terrorist and saw him retreating up the gully.

Decision time. Should he go after the man or rush to Sadria? In the final analysis it wasn't much of a decision; her life took precedence.

Bolan went over the side of the gully in a single bound and raced toward her, the short hairs at his nape tingling at the prospect of receiving a bullet in the back for his effort. He weaved right and left and to his surprise reached her without a shot being fired.

Sadria lay on her right side, the Uzi tucked to her stomach, curled in a fetal position with her eyes closed.

Shifting position so he could keep an eye on the gully and the grounds to the west, Bolan sank to one knee and touched her shoulder. He wanted to roll her onto her back and examine her wounds. As his gaze strayed to her face he detected the faint glistening of moisture under her eyelids.

At the warrior's touch Sadria flinched and gasped, her eyes opening wide in sheer terror. "Mike!"

"Not so loud," Bolan cautioned, realizing she'd been crying and suspecting the reason by her reaction to his touch. "Are you hit?"

Sadria swallowed and shook her head.

"We've got to move," Bolan declared, grabbing her arm and forcefully hauling her upright. He had to hold fast or she would have collapsed; her knees nearly buckled they were trembling so badly.

"I'm scared," she said weakly, sounding amazed. "So scared."

He hooked his left arm around her waist and hurried to where he'd left the duffel, then eased her down so she could sit with her back braced against it while he checked for signs of pursuit.

Suddenly, impulsively, Sadria threw her arms around him and buried her face against his neck. "I'm sorry," she whispered.

As much as Bolan wanted to comfort her, he had a more urgent consideration. He gave her a reassuring hug, waited a minute for her shaking to subside, and said, "We can't stay here."

Sniffling softly, Sadria nodded and let go. "I know."

"Since the house isn't safe we'll have to go farther south," Bolan proposed, helping her to her feet. He slung the duffel over his right shoulder. "Can you manage?"

"Yes" was her barely audible response.

Bolan took her hand and hiked through the trees and undergrowth for another hundred yards until he came to a small grassy clearing surrounding an ancient well, a circular stone affair four feet in height and capped by a rickety wooden roof perched on four severely warped supports. He went around the far side and deposited the duffel, then motioned for Sadria to take a seat.

"I'm sorry," she said again, slumping to the ground.

Moving to the edge of the well, Bolan squatted, gazed through the scope and searched the ground between the well and the house. Not so much as a twig stirred. Apparently they'd given the Black Hand the slip. "What do you have to be sorry about?" he inquired softly.

"You saw me back there. I lost control."

"It's understandable."

"Is it?" Sadria rejoined bitterly. She went on, her voice low, her gaze fixed on the grass near her feet. "I didn't like being left behind. I thought I could prove to you that I can hold my own. So I waited a bit after you went off, then followed."

"You should have stayed put."

"I know that now," Sadria replied. Her next words were spoken in a strained whisper. "There I was, trying to spot you, when all of a sudden someone started firing and the ground around me was being chewed up." She paused. "I was never so scared in my life. I don't know what came over me. My brain wouldn't function and my body began shaking. I fell down. I—I—"

"There's no need to explain," Bolan said. He was tempted to add that now was hardly the proper time, that the terrorists might still be looking for them. Instead he simply told her, "I've got to go back."

Sadria slid over and clutched his arm. "Please don't leave me."

"You'll be all right. Just don't budge," Bolan advised.

"*Please,*" Sadria pleaded. "I don't want to be left alone."

The warrior saw the panic in her face. He knew what he had do, but he couldn't leave her. If she came after him again, she could get them both killed.

At that moment they both stiffened when an automatic weapon shattered the stillness of the night.

AHMET NAIN HAD NEVER known such torment. His body throbbed with pain and every breath he took rasped in his lungs. He wheezed like a hundred-year-old man with asthma and tasted blood in his mouth.

Through sheer willpower he continued to crawl northward toward E23. He dragged the AK-47 with his left hand, although he didn't have the strength to lift it should the government agents catch him. That was his great fear. They'd overtake him and pump more bullets into him to finish him off.

How had it happened? he asked himself. Where had the shots come from that struck him? One second he'd been on top of things, had spotted that woman and shot her, then a hot, searing sensation had lanced through his chest, followed by two more in the blink of an eye, and he'd fallen.

He'd never expected it to happen to him.

Nain had known that most of the band would undoubtedly die violent deaths, but he'd always secretly entertained the notion that the others would be the ones to be slain and he would live out the remainder of his days in seclusion.

What if he died now?

The thought terrified him. For two years he'd dispensed death as casually as any assassin who ever lived. He'd regarded death as a means to an end, as a way of rousing the masses from their intellectual lethargy by shocking them into confronting the reality of economic liberation. Death, the impersonal deaths of countless others, had been but a tool to be used in the ongoing battle against capitalistic imperialism.

But now death had become acutely personal and Ahmet was afraid of what might lie beyond the veil. He concentrated on the gully floor, moving his arms and legs mechanically, and harbored the conviction

that he would be all right if he rejoined his comrades.
They'd know what to do. They'd get a doctor, have
him stitched up and back on his feet in no time.

Ahmet halted in surprise at the sight of a pair of
black shoes blocking his path. Grunting, he craned his
neck and cried out in relief, "Muzo!"

"Not so loud, dear brother," the terrorist said,
crouching and placing a hand on Nain's shoulder.

"I've been hit. You must get me out of here."

Dora looked toward the house. "Where are the
agents?"

"I don't know. Please, let's just get to the car. I
need a doctor badly," Nain said. The front of his shirt
was damp with blood and he began to feel dizzy.

"So I see."

Gritting his teeth, Nain managed to lift his right
hand and extend it. "Here. Help me up."

Instead of complying, Dora simply smiled.

"What are you doing?" Nain demanded, and collapsed in a fit of coughing. Intense waves of agony
racked his body. His mind swirled, overcome by ver-
tigo. For a minute the attack persisted, then abruptly
stopped. He looked at Muza, at that smug smile, and
a chill rippled along his spine.

"From the blood on your lips I would imagine you
are bleeding internally."

"Yes," Nain agreed, and reiterated, "I need a doctor."

Dora thoughtfully pursed his lips. "Not so fast, my
friend."

"I'll die if I don't receive medical attention."

"Probably."

Rage welled within Nain. He tried to swing the AK-47 up and around but the weight was too much for him. The best he could do was move it a few inches.

"Here. Allow me. That must be heavy," Dora said, leaning forward to snatch the gun from Ahmet's hand.

"Why are you doing this?" Nain asked.

"Doing what?"

With all the strength Nain could muster he spit out, "You know damn well what I'm talking about."

Dora tensed and scanned the area. "Must I keep reminding you to keep your voice down? I wouldn't want to be interrupted before we're done."

Tears of frustration formed at the corners of Nain's eyes. He placed his left cheek on the hard ground and said weakly, "You bastard. Get it over with."

"Why rush?" Dora responded. "I don't see any sign of Arpinar's storm troopers, and there are a few things we must make clear."

"Screw you."

"There's nothing personal in this."

"Liar."

Shifting position, Dora braced his back against the west bank and alertly watched for the government agents while talking in a low, soothing voice. "You have never understood the total picture, Ahmet. Just between the two of us, you're a selfish son of a bitch. Your decision to desert us confirms it."

Nain said nothing.

"If you were as devoted to the cause as the rest of us, you would never dream of leaving. But you're thinking only of yourself. You've placed your needs above any loyalty to the Black Hand that you once possessed," Dora said. "It's sad to see how far you've fallen."

"Do it, damn you."

"Soon, brother. Soon. Don't rush me." Dora deposited the Uzi on the ground at his feet and held the AK-47 in both hands. "When I told you this isn't personal, I wasn't lying. It's a matter of professional ethics. You swore an oath, remember? If I was to let you leave, then the others would view their own oaths as meaningless. They might develop similar ideas about leaving. The Black Hand would cease to exist."

Nain lifted his head. "I pray that you burn in hell forever."

"Oh? Do you want my company down there?"

"If I could, I would strangle you."

Sighing, Dora tucked the AK-47's stock under his right arm and trained the barrel on his prostrate friend. "It's obvious I am wasting my time. Any final thoughts before you embrace eternity?"

"Yes," Nain stated harshly. "You won't be able to fool the others indefinitely. Eventually they'll realize that they mean nothing to you. All your talk of comradeship and loyalty has been a pack of lies. You've called me selfish for wanting out of the constant killing, but at least I'm not like you. I'm not sick. I don't enjoy it."

Dora moved the AK-47's barrel in a small circle. "So you think I like to kill just for the sheer joy of it?" He chuckled. "Do you know what? You're right." His finger tightened on the trigger, and the assault rifle thundered and bucked, but he held the barrel steady and watched coldly as Nain's eyes and forehead were blasted into bits and pieces. He kept firing until the

weapon went empty, stitching holes from one end of
Nain to the other, seeing the body jerk and thrash. At
last he tossed the AK-47 aside, grabbed the Uzi and
raced off toward the car.

17

"Who were they shooting at?" Sadria wondered aloud after the echoes of the gunfire died away.

"I don't know," Bolan said quietly, puzzled by the incident. The weapon had been an AK-47, perhaps the same one used by the killer in the gully. Which meant the man must still be alive. But why had the guy opened up? "I'm going to go check."

Sadria squeezed his arm. "I don't want to be left here by myself."

"You'll be all right," the warrior assured her. "I promise I won't be gone long."

Although clearly loath to do so, Sadria released him and leaned against the well, the Uzi in her lap. "Go ahead."

"We'll talk more when I get back," Bolan promised. "Stay down and don't go anywhere this time."

"You don't need to worry on that score."

With a nod Bolan was up and running, heading through the trees in the direction of the gully. His acute combat senses probed his surroundings and failed to register any hostile presence. Every thirty feet he stopped to use the night scope.

He slowed when he neared the gully and double-checked its rim before sprinting across the remaining distance and sliding to the bottom. Crouching, he listened for the telltale sounds of furtive movement that would signify they'd seen him and were converging on his position, but all his ears detected was the breeze and the rustling of the brush and tree limbs.

Even more mystified, Bolan advanced cautiously up the gully. He saw no one near or in the house, no one in the field out front. Using the scope every five seconds, he advanced well past the point where he'd shot either Dora or Nain and halted abruptly when he saw the body blocking his way.

The warrior froze, studying the corpse, verifying that not a spark of life remained. The scope's magnification enhanced the grisly ruin of the man's face and the dozens of holes oozing blood.

Bolan inched closer, his mind awhirl with the implications. From the clothes it appeared to be the guy he'd shot. Someone had done him a favor and finished the guy off. But who? Why? He stopped next to the man's feet and tried to logically determine the answers.

From the guy's size it had to be Nain. There wasn't enough of the face intact for a positive identification, but the body couldn't be more than five-feet-ten and Muzaffer Dora was much taller, Bolan's height but slimmer. Evidently Dora or even Yeni Yurukoglu had finished Nain off. Why?

Bolan scanned the area once more, then picked up the AK-47 and verified that the magazine was empty. He slung the weapon over his left shoulder and resumed searching for the terrorists, going all the way to E23 without seeing any sign of them. A sweep of the field and a check of the house confirmed that Dora and Yurukoglu were indeed gone.

The return to the well took no time at all and Bolan saw Sadria in the exact spot where he'd left her, gazing blankly off into space. Kneeling, he placed a hand on her shoulder. She started and glanced at him.

"Mike! I didn't hear you come up."

"Sorry. Old habits are hard to break," Bolan said.

"Did you find the terrorists?"

"I found Ahmet Nain dead. The others are gone."

"So what next?" Sadria asked.

"We can try to hitch a ride or spend the night in the house," Bolan proposed.

"Do you think the house is safe?"

"It should be. I'll make another sweep of the grounds to be sure, though."

"I can collect some branches and we could make a small fire," Sadria proposed.

"Let's do it."

They returned to the old dwelling. Sadria gave the Uzi to Bolan and gathered a bundle of sticks and branches. Once back in the living room Bolan placed the duffel and the AK-47 in a corner, set the Uzi on top and started to leave.

"Mike."

He paused and looked at her.

"Thanks again for saving my life."

"My pleasure," Bolan said. He nodded at the pile of limbs. "Don't start the fire until I get back."

"Yes, sir," she said sweetly.

Twenty minutes were required for a complete circuit of the surrounding area. Bolan checked every possible place of concealment, probing behind every thicket, boulder and tree, but found no trace of the terrorists. Convinced they had definitely departed, he entered the house and saw Sadria kneeling in the center of the room. "We're all alone," he announced.

"Good," she said huskily, looking up at him.

"Are you all right?" Bolan asked, going over and kneeling in front of her.

"Fine," Sadria stated. She reached up and gently placed a hand on each side of his neck.

"We can get that fire going now if you'd like to keep warm."

Sadria shook her head. "There are other ways of keeping warm." She leaned closer and tenderly pressed her lips against his.

Bolan let the M-16 slide from his grasp. Her lips and tongue were intoxicating, arousing him. He touched her waist and felt her trembling. Slowly, almost tentatively, his right hand strayed higher and cupped her breast. She moaned and fused her body to his. Together they sank to the floor, and for a brief interval each became the center of the other's universe.

For the first time in many years the old house was filled with soft sounds other than those made by the breeze.

"POOR AHMET," Dora said with just the right amount of sorrow in his tone. He bowed his head.

Yeni, her knuckles white on the steering wheel, gave him a sympathetic glance. "It must have been terrible."

"It was," Dora agreed. "I'm only glad you weren't there to see what they did to him."

"Tell me."

"I can't. It's too horrible." Dora faced the window and sagged against the door.

"Please. I heard the firing. I almost got out and came to help."

"It's a good thing you didn't. They might have killed you, too."

"Did you see them kill him?"

"No," Dora said. "I got there too late. Ahmet was lying on his stomach in a pool of blood. He had been shot to pieces."

"The sadistic bastards!"

"That's not the worst part. It was obvious they shot him in the back."

"Damn them!" Yeni spat. "You should have avenged his death."

Dora glanced at her. "Don't you think I wanted to kill them? But they outnumbered me three to one and they had taken cover in a gully. There was no way I could get close without being spotted." He paused, struck by inspiration. "Besides, I overheard them talking. They had a radio in their car and called for assistance before the crash. Reinforcements were on the way. For all I knew two carloads of government agents might have arrived at any second."

Yeni fell silent.

Pleased at his performance, Dora leaned his head back on the top of the seat. "We must pay them back very soon."

"There's always the NATO conference."

"Indeed. Arpinar will have his people posted all over the Hilton. We can, as the Americans like to say, kill two birds with one stone."

"Who will handle the explosives with Ahmet gone?" Yeni inquired.

"We'll manage by ourselves. We might not possess Ahmet's expertise, but we can set a timer properly."

"Wait until Orhan and Nur hear the news," Yeni said sadly. "Orhan will be furious."

"No doubt," Dora agreed, and decided to try to take her mind off the traitor's death. "Mind if I turn on the radio?"

"Go right ahead."

Flicking it on, Dora worked the dial until he found a station in Izmir playing upbeat songs. He relaxed, placed his hands behind his head and closed his eyes. The trip to Usak had gone well. Not only had he evened the score with Vahdettin, he'd destroyed a police station and slain a number of cops in the bargain. Killing Ahmet had been the icing on the cake. The fool! He wanted to laugh, thinking of how stupid Ahmet had been. Nain would have been smarter to simply disappear instead of announcing his intention to quit the Black Hand in advance.

For almost half an hour they drove steadily westward. No further sign of pursuit materialized. The music ended and an announcer stated that the hourly newscast was next.

"Find something else," Yeni suggested. "I don't want to listen to news."

Drowsing and on the verge of falling asleep, Dora came sluggishly awake. "What?"

"I'd rather not listen to the news," Yeni reiterated.

"Perhaps we should," Dora said, struggling to get his mind in gear. "There might be a report on our attack at Usak."

A deep-voiced newsman came on the air with the lead headline: "A gun battle took place this evening on the streets of Izmir between authorities and members of the notorious terrorist gang known as the Black Hand. Details in a moment."

Dora sat up straight, barely hearing the commercial that came on. "Members. He said members. That means both Orhan and Nur were involved."

"But what could have gone wrong?" Yeni wondered, slowing and staring in dread at the radio.

The newsman came back on. "Two American tourists taken captive by the Black Hand were freed this evening when members of the Terrorism Department and Izmir police raided the apartment on Topkapi Street where they were being held. Two terrorists were in the apartment at the time. One, identified as Nur Yazici, was slain. The other, believed to be Orhan Mithat, escaped. Tragically five police officers were killed and Mehmet Arpinar, the director of the justice ministry's counterterrorism division, was wounded. He is listed in stable condition at Bahribaba Hospital."

"Nur dead!" Yeni exclaimed, horrified. "No, it can't be!"

A peculiar numbness seized Dora. He gaped blankly at the dial, unwilling to believe what had happened.

"In a related story," the newsman went on, "there is word from Ankara that the son of a prominent judge has been arrested as an accomplice in the Black Hand's criminal activities. Details are still sketchy, but Tashin Pamir is alleged to have funneled funds to the terrorists."

Yeni abruptly pulled the car over to the shoulder and braked. "They have Tashin," she said softly, stunned.

The announcer drifted into other stories concerning a three-vehicle accident on Gazi Bulvari and a house fire that had claimed the lives of a family of seven.

"What do we do?" Yeni asked, looking at Muzo.

"I don't know," he snapped, rousing from his shock, a finely tempered rage seeping into every pore of his body. He flicked off the radio in disgust and pounded the dashboard.

"How did they find out about Tashin?" Yeni wanted to know. "I thought our apartment in Izmir was safe. You told us it was. How did they learn about it?"

"Quiet," Dora barked. "I need to think." He tapped his fingers on the dash, his brow furrowed, and reasoned aloud. "Since we used phony names to rent the apartment, the only way the authorities could have found out about it was through Tashin. Somehow they learned of his link to us and made him talk." He frowned. "I knew we should never have taken the fool into our confidence."

"What choice did we have?" Yeni responded. "We needed his money."

"This will make us look like idiots," Dora declared.

"Is that all you can think of? What about Nur?"

Dora glowered at her. "How dare you. You know how I felt about her. What do you want me to do? Scream, rave and cry? I'd rather get even."

"What do we do now?"

"We head for our safehouse in Istanbul."

"Why there?"

"Think, woman, think. That's where Orhan will go. It's the only refuge we have left," Dora said. His eyes narrowed. "Did you ever give the address of our Istanbul safehouse to that pig Pamir?"

"No. Absolutely not. I followed your instructions to the letter," Yeni said. "He wouldn't have known about our apartment in Izmir, either, if you hadn't told me to invite him there for that boring weekend I spent in bed with him."

"We had to keep him hooked," Dora said. "You were the only bait we had."

"There was always Nur," Yeni said resentfully.

"He didn't like her."

"Lucky Nur."

Dora sighed. "If it bothers you so much, don't talk about it."

For all of ten seconds neither spoke a word.

"He did know the phone number to our Istanbul place though," Yeni said, breaking the uncomfortable silence. "He called there a dozen or more times. I'd directed him to always place his calls from pay phones, so I doubt the police could ever trace them."

"Good," Dora said, nodding. "Then we still have one factor in our favor. We'll find Orhan and make our plans for the future."

"What about the NATO summit?"

"What about it?"

"We can't hit it now."

"Why can't we?" Dora countered. "The three of us are more than enough to do the job properly. I'm not about to call off such a great opportunity to bring international attention to our cause. If we succeed we'll make headlines around the world."

"And if we don't?"

"We'll still make headlines."

18

Orhan Mithat strolled along the sidewalk behind
Bahribaba Hospital, his hands buried in the pockets
of his pants, the perfect picture of innocence. As he
walked he could feel the shoulder holster containing
the Walther PPK/S rubbing against his side under his
blue jacket. Snug in a back pocket was a Wilson Arms
sound suppressor.

Immediately after the fight in the park with the big
man wearing the overcoat, Mithat had reluctantly
ditched the Gustav in a flower garden and made his
way to the train station. Instead of taking a train, he
went to the locker Nur had rented months earlier under an alias and used his key to retrieve certain items
kept there for just such a contingency. In his front
pocket was a new set of false identification papers
forged by a master in the illicit trade. And in addition
to the Walther, he also had a stiletto strapped to his
right leg above the ankle.

Mithat came to the corner, checked to make sure
there were no cops stationed on the east side of the
hospital, then reversed direction, whistling softly.
He'd been all set to head for Istanbul, had even pur-
chased a ticket for the next Izmir to Istanbul express.
Then fortune smiled on him. He'd gone across the

street from the station to enjoy a few beers at a tavern before the express departed and heard a news bulletin on the radio behind the bar.

Now he stopped directly behind Bahribaba Hospital and stared up at the seven-story structure. Somewhere in there was the illustrious Mehmet Arpinar, the man responsible for Nur's death, the man who had vowed to hound the Black Hand until every last one of them was dead.

Somewhere up there was the son of a bitch Mithat intended to kill.

He ambled toward a door, passing a trash bin and a bicycle chained to a rail. He tried the knob, found it unlocked and slipped inside. An empty white corridor extended for a dozen yards. There were several doors on either side. He moved warily forward, found a utility closet on the right and a linen closet on the left. At the next doorway he peered into a staff lounge occupied by a single man dressed in a white lab coat who was seated at a long table and sipping a cup of coffee.

Ducking back, Mithat retraced his steps to the utility closet and stepped inside. It took but a few seconds to attach the sound suppressor to the Walther, which he then held under his jacket as he returned to the staff room and went in. "Hello," he said amiably.

The man glanced around, curiosity lining his features, the coffee cup midway to his lips. "May I help you?"

He smiled and walked nearer. "Would you be so kind as to help me find the room I'm looking for?"

"It's well after visiting hours," the man noted. "You should come back tomorrow."

Mithat halted at arm's length from his unsuspecting victim and shook his head, still smiling. "You don't understand. I'm with the Izmir police and I'm supposed to deliver some papers to Mehmet Arpinar."

"At this hour?"

Shrugging, the terrorist chuckled. "A policeman's work is never done."

"I know what you mean. But you should try being a doctor sometime. I just spent two hours in surgery working to save the leg of a man injured in that accident on Gazi Bulvari. Earlier, I operated on your Mr. Arpinar." He began to lower the cup. "The director is in Room 303."

"Thank you."

Depositing the cup in a saucer, the doctor glanced up. "I hope these papers are important enough to justify disturbing him. He really shouldn't be bothered."

"See for yourself," Mithat offered cordially, whipping out the Walther.

The doctor stiffened and his mouth started to widen.

Mithat squeezed the trigger three times. The sound suppressor coughed softly as three rounds were pumped into the physician's brow. The man's head snapped back, then sagged onto his chest. Quickly the terrorist hooked his hands under the doctor's arms and dragged him to the doorway. A hasty check revealed that the corridor was still empty.

Backpedaling, Mithat lugged the body to the utility closet and propped it against the rear wall. He left the door open a crack, stuck the Walther under his belt and stripped off the white lab coat. The sleeves were too long, so he folded the cuffs back.

He walked to the end of the hall and peeked out the door. Except for a nurse at her duty station off to the right, the hallway beyond was empty.

Mithat's grin widened. This was working out far better than he'd dared hope. Praise God that hospitals were minimally staffed after midnight! And since the complacent police obviously didn't expect an attempt to be made on Arpinar's life, there appeared to be no guards.

How accommodating of them.

Giving the Walther a tap, Mithat adjusted the lab coat to hide it and went in search of a stairwell.

MEHMET ARPINAR COULDN'T sleep. Despite the painkillers and the heavy medication, he lay in his bed staring up at the white ceiling, his mind racing, reviewing the events of the day. Of all the stupid mistakes to make, being shot had to rank as number one. By the next morning everyone in Turkey would know about his humiliation.

How strange Fate worked sometimes. Had his reflexes been a shade faster, had he used his head instead of stupidly trying to take Orhan Mithat alive, he would be a hero now instead of a sheep's ass.

Arpinar twisted his neck and gazed at the sheaf of papers lying on the nightstand. At least he had a clue to work with thanks to the two men who worked in Hasan's section; his death had spurred them to diligently double-check the telephone company's records of phone calls made from the Pamir residence for the past two years and their persistence had paid off.

Too bad he couldn't act on the information himself. According to Dr. Olcay he would be stuck in the hospital for two weeks, possibly three, which meant he would miss the NATO summit in Ankara.

A twinge in his abdomen made Arpinar grunt, and he closed his eyes as he plotted his next move. The information should be given to Belasko, he decided. He recalled how intensely he'd resented the idea of working with the man. Yet now he was prepared to rely on Belasko instead of his own people.

Why?

The answer was simple. Belasko would get the job done right. He'd grown to admire the American. There was an indefinable quality the man possessed, something in his eyes and the way he carried himself, that suggested supreme competence.

Arpinar had known a great many intelligence operatives, military men and police officers in his time, and none had aroused in him the same respect as Belasko. He recalled the time he'd visited an army base and observed a unit of elite Turkish commandos going through their paces. In a way Belasko reminded him of them—men who gave one hundred percent every minute of every day, men who had been pushed to the limits of their endurance again and again and always met the challenge, men who were preeminent in combat.

He felt fatigue gnawing at his mind and yawned. Maybe he would finally get some rest. Ten or twelve hours would make a new man out of him. Drifting into that vague twilight bordering on slumber, he heard a strange sound, the faintest of popping noises came from the hallway outside his room.

Almost out, Arpinar struggled to revive, his eyelids fluttering. The popping had been familiar, a distinctive noise he'd heard on several occasions during the course of his career. But it couldn't be true. His mind had to be playing tricks on him. Or so he thought until his eyes snapped open and he saw the person standing at the foot of his bed, grinning.

"Hello, Mr. Arpinar," Orhan Mithat said.

Stunned, Arpinar tried to prop himself on his elbows.

The terrorist's right hand swept up. In it was a small pistol fitted with a sound suppressor. "Don't exert yourself on my account."

The dark hole in the end of the suppressor was like the baleful orb of a Cyclops, mesmerizing the director, riveting him in place. He tried to speak, but his vocal chords wouldn't cooperate.

Evidently enjoying the situation, Mithat chuckled and wagged the pistol. "Don't bother calling for the officer they had watching your room. He's dead."

Arpinar wished he had the strength to leap on the bastard, to take a wild swing, to do anything other than lie there and be helplessly slaughtered.

"And don't bother ringing for the duty nurse," Mithat added. "She's leaking blood all over her desk even as we speak."

"Scum!" Arpinar finally exploded.

"Not very original. I expected better from you. After all, you're the darling of the press, the man who will single-handedly wipe out every terrorist in Turkey. You're the best there is at what you do."

Arpinar groaned and managed to raise the upper portion of his body a few inches above the bed. His face turned red, the veins in his neck bulging. "Get it over with, you son of a bitch."

"What's the rush? I have a minute to kill." He tittered at his play on words.

"I only regret I won't be here to see Belasko get you," Arpinar said resentfully.

"Who?"

"You'll find out," Arpinar predicted.

"Belasko isn't a Turkish name. Is he the one who chased me earlier? Although I didn't see him clearly the man didn't appear to be Turkish. And if not for a tree limb your Belasko would be in bits and pieces right now. He's not worth worrying about."

"Keep telling yourself that until you are six feet under," Arpinar taunted, trying to gird himself to make a frantic lunge. The wound and the medication conspired to provoke a woozy feeling.

"I hope you appreciate all the trouble I went to in paying you this visit," Mithat said in mock seriousness. "It's been fun, but I must go."

Arpinar braced for what was coming.

"Since I didn't bring any flowers, you'll have to settle for these," the terrorist said, and fired twice.

An intense burning sensation lanced through Arpinar's chest and he collapsed, in shock, still alive and able to hear the terrorist's scornful laughter as it faded down the hallway. He attempted to push up again, but his arms weighed a ton. The beating of his heart reminded him of the booming of a bass drum, growing louder and louder until it seemed on the verge of exploding.

Then it did.

19

Bahribaba Hospital swarmed with police and government men when Mack Bolan and Sadria Inonu arrived the next morning at ten o'clock. She presented her identification to a pair of officers stationed at the entrance and questioned them in Turkish.

Bolan saw the shock on her face when one of them replied. He followed her into the spacious lobby, where dozens of reporters were clustered, and took hold of her arm. "What is it?"

"Mehmet," Sadria said in a daze. "He's dead."

"From the wounds he sustained at the apartment?" Bolan asked, surprised.

"No. He was murdered last night in his hospital bed," Sadria disclosed, then swallowed hard, on the verge of losing her self-control.

A beefy reporter in need of a shave spotted her and detached himself from the pack of news hounds. "Miss Inonu," he called out and went on in Turkish as he approached.

Bolan had a natural dislike of most members of the media. Sadria was numb, in no condition to be pestered by an arrogant member of the fourth estate, and even though Bolan couldn't understand what the guy was saying, he knew the tone well enough. Off to the left was a stairwell. Bolan discreetly propelled her toward it and got there a good ten feet ahead of the reporter. Once inside he paused to see if the man would follow. The man didn't.

Sadria leaned against the wall. "Not Mehmet," she said softly.

"You've got to snap out of it," Bolan advised, placing the duffel at his feet. He gripped her shoulders and gave her a little shake. "I can imagine how you feel, but now isn't the time or place to let yourself go. Do you understand?"

She looked at him and seemed to reach deep down inside herself. Nodding, she mustered a wan smiled and said, "Sorry. This on top of everything else I've been through in the past twenty-four hours really got to me. It won't happen again. Let's find out what happened." Sadria headed up the stairs.

Grabbing the duffel, the warrior stayed at her side all the way to the third floor. The moment they emerged a lean man in a brown suit spotted her and hurried over.

"Sadria," the man said, extending his hands.

She took them, squeezed and spoke rapidly in Turkish. He answered readily, casting frequent glances at the big man beside her.

After a minute Sadria turned to Bolan. "Where are my manners? Mike, this is Nuri Yildirim. He works in my department. I'm afraid he doesn't speak much English."

"Merhaba," Bolan said and shook hands.

Yildirim talked with Sadria for a while, then hurried toward the room where most of the activity was centered.

"The director was not the only one killed," Sadria told Bolan. "A doctor, two nurses and a police officer were also brutally murdered, shot in the head several times each."

"Any clues as to who did it?"

"Not yet. I would blame the Black Hand except that we know where they were at the time Mehmet was slain."

"We don't know where all of them were," Bolan noted. "Orhan Mithat got away from us at the apartment, remember? I didn't see any sign of him in Usak, so this could have been his work."

"Mithat? Yes, he's the type to commit such an atrocity," Sadria commented. "Perhaps he wanted revenge for the raid and heard that Mehmet had been brought to this hospital."

"What will you do now?"

"*We* are going to take the next plane to Istanbul."

"Why there?"

"I'll show you in a second," Sadria said.

Yildirim came out of the room holding a sheaf of papers in his left hand. He quickly passed them over.

"We might have hit the jackpot," Sadria said, taking the papers. "Listed here is every phone call made from the Pamir residence since the Black Hand first formed. Our people found an Istanbul phone number listed only once. They contacted the Istanbul police department and detectives were sent to check on the address." Her lips curved in a grin.

"And?" Bolan prompted.

"The house is an isolated affair near an old cemetery. A discreet investigation uncovered that it was rented by a young couple, a pair of supposed newlyweds. From the descriptions provided to the detectives, the newlyweds were Nur Yazici and Orhan Mithat.''

"Did the detectives go near the house?"

"Absolutely not. They were under strict orders to do no more than drive past it."

Yildirim interjected a few comments.

"Will you excuse me for a minute, Mike?" Sadria asked. "There are some minor matters I must take care of and then we can leave."

"Go right ahead."

The two Turks moved off, deep in a discussion.

Hoping she wouldn't take too long, Bolan strolled down the corridor until he came to 303. Except for curious stares, none of the agents or officers paid any attention to him. Each had a job to do and went about it efficiently. Two men were using tape to lift dirt and hair samples from the floor. Others were dusting for prints.

Bolan stared at the bed, surprised to see Arpinar's body still lying there. The director's face was frozen in a troubled expression, and bloodstains had dried on the man's hospital gown.

"Pardon me."

Pivoting, Bolan found a young man in a gray suit studying him intently. "What can I do for you?"

"I am Dursun. I work in the Terrorism Department. You are Belasko, yes?"

"That's right," Bolan confirmed.

"My English not so good. I want to say I talk with the director yesterday after he was shot," Dursun said, his forehead creased in concentration as he tried to find the right words. "He spoke on you."

Bolan patiently waited.

"He said he like you very much. Call you *arkadas*. Understand?"

"What does that mean?"

"Friend," Dursun translated. "Thought you would like to know." He turned and walked off.

Walking to the side of the bed, Bolan stared into Arpinar's glazed eyes. Friend, the man had said. How many of those had the warrior lost over the years? Certainly more than he cared to dwell on. Lasting friendships were a rarity in his profession.

"Mike?"

Bolan looked around.

Sadria stood at the foot of the bed. "Are you ready to leave?"

"You're all done here?" Bolan inquired.

"Yildirim has everything well in hand. He'll keep me posted on any developments," the woman replied, then gestured at the doorway. Her gaze lingered on Arpinar before she ventured out.

"How many of your people are going with us?" the big man asked as they made for the stairs.

"None," Sadria said gruffly. "One of our agents is already in Istanbul, and we'll have the complete cooperation of the Istanbul police."

Bolan received the odd impression she was holding something back, but he didn't pry. "Shouldn't you have your head wound checked while we're here?"

"I don't have time."

"How about if I insist?" Bolan said, grabbing her arm.

"I'm fine. The gash is sore, that's all."

"Humor me."

"You're worse than my mother. All right. If it will make you happy."

Frowning, Sadria walked toward a woman in a white uniform. "This shouldn't take more than two or three minutes."

Actually it took fifteen. Bolan was leaning against the wall when she finally returned sporting a white bandage over the wound. "Well?"

"Thanks to you I now have five stitches. Now let's go."

They grabbed a taxi, and twenty minutes later were at the Adnan Menderes Airport, boarding one of the six daily flights between Izmir and Istanbul offered by Turkish Airlines. As a government agent Sadria could carry weapons, and arranged for Bolan's duffel to be stored in a closet aft of the cabin.

"The flight will take about an hour," she informed the big man.

Bolan settled back in his window seat and waited until after the aircraft rumbled off the runway and banked in a wide loop to the north before bringing up a pertinent point. "You're now the head of the Terrorist Department, aren't you?"

"Temporarily. I'm sure a new one will be appointed in a week or two."

"Maybe it'll be you."

A short laugh was her response.

"Why not? You're the logical choice."

"Politics, my dear Mike. Politics. Our president will want a man, a tough law-and-order type like Mehmet who can stir the press and the people with his fierce scowl."

"Your sarcasm is showing again."

"Can you blame me?"

"No, I guess not," Bolan said, and then got to the real point. "How does Arpinar's death affect my status here?"

"It doesn't," Sadria stated. "Instead of working with him, you will now work with me."

"And what about the Black Hand? What kind of approach will you take?"

Sadria glanced at him. "Oh. I see. You're concerned I might insist that we take them alive."

"Something like that."

"You have no need to worry. After Usak and the ambush on E23 I began to question whether adhering to the legal niceties was practical. Mehmet's murder finally made up my mind for me."

"Meaning?"

"Meaning that when we arrive in Istanbul, with your consent I'm going to point you in the terrorists' direction and let you tear them apart."

20

Istanbul, Turkey. Once known as magnificent Constantinople, a rival of mighty Rome. Now a sea of tightly packed buildings swarming with nearly three million inhabitants.

Seated in the back seat of a car winding its way up a hill in the Tesvikiye section of the sprawling metropolis, Bolan gazed out the rear window to see if they were being tailed and enjoyed a panoramic view stretching down to the Bosporus, the narrow strait separating Asia from Europe. The sun had set an hour earlier and the lights of the city were ablaze.

''We should be there soon,'' Sadria announced.

Bolan swung around. She sat in the front on the passenger side. Behind the wheel was an agent named Husnu, a stocky, laconic sort who spoke little English and gave the impression of regarding the warrior's presence as favorably as he might the bubonic plague.

They were driving in a northeasterly direction past low-rent apartments and homes of the lower middle class. Despite the late hour they passed a couple of street vendors, one hawking bottled water, the other ice cream. The farther and higher they went, the fewer pedestrians they encountered until finally there were none.

"There's the cemetery," Sadria announced, pointing ahead and to the left.

Situated on the crest of the hill, the two-acre burial tract was ringed on three sides by fields. An ancient rusted wrought-iron fence, largely overgrown with weeds and vines, surrounded the site. Crumbling tombstones and several decrepit mausoleums marked the final resting places of individuals long since gone.

Bolan surveyed the cemetery carefully, then shifted his attention to the one-story house on the right side of the road, a structure precariously perched on the very rim of the hill.

"That is the house," Sadria verified.

An ideal spot, Bolan mentally noted. Below it was a short, steep slope devoid of homes. To the north and south vacant lots choked with weeds and debris were adequate buffer zones. Windows on every side afforded the terrorists an unobstructed field of fire. During daylight hours no one could approach without being seen. Nighttime wouldn't be much better if someone inside had night-vision gear.

Sadria leaned forward. "There's someone home."

So it appeared. Bolan noticed a light on in every room and one on the front porch. But no shadows moved across the shades that had been drawn over the windows. If there was someone in there, he wasn't moving around.

The road passed between the cemetery and the house, and the driver started to slow as they drew abreast of the building.

"Don't," Bolan warned. "Maintain your speed."

Sadria quickly relayed the instructions and Husnu belatedly complied.

Bolan kept his eyes on the windows. The sudden deceleration might have aroused the curiosity of any occupants.

Seconds later one of the shades moved slightly, revealing a hand and a forearm.

"Damn," Bolan muttered. Someone was watching their taillights recede down the hill.

"What's the matter?"

Bolan told her. He saw the arm withdraw and the shade hung evenly once again.

"I don't think it is anything to worry about," Sadria said. "Cars use this road regularly to get from Macka Street to Nuzhetiye Street."

"I guess you're right," Bolan said, still eyeing the windows.

They were nearing the bottom of the hill. The road angled to the right and into a residential neighborhood.

"Have Husnu swing in a wide circle and go past the house again," Bolan instructed her. "And make sure he doesn't slow down this time."

It took them ten minutes to make the loop around the hill, Husnu sticking to the side streets most of the way. Another car preceded them up the road and another was several car-lengths behind.

Bolan liked being sandwiched in the middle. Should any of the terrorists look out a window, they would simply see a string of traffic passing by and be less inclined to view the vehicles with suspicion. He concentrated on the cemetery again, plotting his approach route, leaving as little to chance as possible.

None of the shades moved as the three cars drove by. Bolan studied the vacant lots, deciding whether to approach from the north or the south, and it was then that he spotted the squat outline of a sedan parked in deep shadows at the east edge of the north lot, apparently deliberately placed as far back from the road as possible. Was it the green car?

"It's not too late to change your mind," Sadria said. "I would be more than happy to have a squad of police handle this if you'd rather not go in."

"This is what I do best," Bolan told her. "I'll go." He reached under his lightweight overcoat and adjusted his utility belts, then picked up the Uzi from the seat beside him. "Pull over on the left shoulder at the bottom of the hill just before the road cuts to the right."

Sadria relayed the command. She gazed at the warrior, her face pale in the subdued light, her eyes conveying her concern. "Do you still want us to wait an hour before we return with reinforcements?"

"Yes," Bolan confirmed, checking that the Desert Eagle rode securely on his right hip and the Beretta was held fast in its shoulder holster.

"Sixty minutes is a long time. If something happens to you, we won't know until well after the fact."

"Can't be helped," Bolan informed her. "I'm not about to barge in there. It'll be half an hour to forty minutes before I make my move."

The car was almost to the curve.

Sadria addressed Husnu and he began to slow the vehicle. She glanced at the big man and grinned self-consciously. "You look like a cannibal in that war paint of yours."

"Combat cosmetics keep the skin from glistening," Bolan said absently, scanning the road ahead. Thankfully there was no oncoming traffic.

"I just hope you don't bump into anyone in the dark. You might give them a heart attack."

Bolan gripped the door handle. He knew her comments were meant to disguise her apprehension. "I'll try not to scare any of the locals to death," he promised, his eyes on the opposite shoulder.

"Mike—" Sadria began.

But the time for conversation had ended. Husnu flicked on the turn signal, slanted across the other lane and braked at the edge of the field that led to the cemetery.

Waiting until the trailing vehicle went by, Bolan flung open the door and vaulted from the seat. He shoved the door shut as he cleared the car. Landing on his right shoulder he rolled into the waist-high weeds.

Husnu floored the gas pedal and the car sped off.

Staying prone, Bolan made certain no vehicles were coming from either direction before he rose into a crouch and hurried deeper into the field. He covered twenty yards before altering his course toward the cemetery.

The ground inclined sharply. Bolan saw headlight beams play over the top of the hill, and a car appeared. Even though he was well out of the range of the twin beams and doubted anyone could see him from the road, he paused and squatted until the car had gone a hundred yards past him.

The nearer he drew to the cemetery, the slower he went. He couldn't ask for a better place from which to observe the house. The tombstones, mausoleums and

neglected vegetation afforded ample hiding spots. Not
that he had much of a choice. Approaching the house
from the east, up the steep, almost-barren slope, had
been out of the question. And the vacant lots, while
thick with weeds, were bordered by other houses. This
way was the best.

Bolan came to the fence. The iron bars were spaced
six inches apart and tipped with triangular barbs.
Close up, the vines weren't as closely spaced as they'd
appeared from the road. He looped the Uzi's shoulder strap over his left arm, gripped two bars and
hauled himself upward. At the top he slowly eased
over the barbs, holding his body parallel to the
ground, and dropped lightly into the cemetery.

He shrugged off a fleeting creepy feeling as he pad-
ded among the tombstones toward the road. A heavy
gate, closed and padlocked, hung directly across from
the terrorists' house. The thick high grass at its base
would conceal him perfectly.

A mausoleum loomed on the left, its sides chipped
and cracked. He glided along its north wall, in the
darkest shadow, and halted shy of the corner to sur-
vey the area. Clearly no one had been buried in the
cemetery for many, many years, and the padlock indicated none would be in the future. Perhaps, given
the continuing urban sprawl of the spreading metropolis, the cemetery was doomed to be razed to make
way for more apartment buildings or homes. He went
to step into the open.

Someone coughed to his left.

The Executioner crouched and froze, his senses
reaching out to probe the night and identify the

source. The cougher was close, perhaps in front of the mausoleum. Placing his left palm on the ground, Bolan leaned forward and risked a peek.

Narrow marble columns supported a peaked overhang. In the middle of the wall stood the door, ajar a good foot. From inside came another cough.

The warrior's logical mind weighed possibilities and calculated probabilities. From the sound he deduced the person to be a man. Could it be one of the terrorists? Not very likely, he decided. There was no reason for any of the Black Hand to be in the cemetery; if they were going to post a guard outside, they would do so closer to the house, in one of the lots.

It must be a local, Bolan figured. Perhaps a vagrant temporarily living in the mausoleum. Or a grave robber. An even slimmer likelihood was someone else had an interest in the Black Hand and was spying on the house from inside the crypt. All of the possibilities spelled potential trouble. He couldn't afford an unknown element at his back while he attended to business.

He ran his left hand over the soil until he found a small stone. Cupping it, he straightened. Perhaps he could draw out whoever was in there, using the most basic of ruses. With a quick toss he flung the stone against a column near the door, then stepped back.

The stone struck the marble with a loud crack and clattered against the wall.

A muffled exclamation within confirmed the mystery man had heard the noise.

Bolan listened to shuffling footsteps and peered out again.

Standing a yard from the doorway, his hands on his narrow hips, was a scruffy man in shabby attire, a nasty scowl on his face. He glanced around, puzzled.

Bolan knew the guy had to be neutralized. He couldn't take the chance, however slight, of the guy spotting him, noticing the weapons and running off to notify the police, which could bring unsuspecting officers in a patrol car to the cemetery and alarm the terrorists. A simple tap on the jaw should do the trick.

The man turned left and right. *"Bu kim?"* he asked nervously.

Bolan transferred the Uzi to his left hand, pressed his back to the mausoleum and stamped his foot several times. He counted on the dull thuds bringing the man to the corner. Sure enough, they did. But what he didn't count on was that the guy would be holding a long, slender knife, and would swing into view with the blade already slashing at his chest.

21

From the surprised expression the man wore, the stroke appeared to be a lucky fluke. He'd jumped around the corner with the intention of discovering what had made the noises, extending his arms protectively.

Fluke or not, Bolan had a heartbeat to react. He flung himself to the right and felt the tip of the blade rip through his coat and dig into one of the pouches on his harness. Instantly he reversed momentum, pivoting and planting a haymaker that lifted the Turk from his feet and crumpled the man in a heap next to a column.

Inserting a finger in the inch-long slit in his coat, Bolan found the knife had struck a pouch containing spare clips for the Beretta. A couple of inches either way and he'd be breathing blood.

He saw the knife on the ground and took the precaution of hiding it behind a nearby tombstone before advancing under cover to the fence bordering the road. A car roared up the hill as he flattened, sinking into a patch of tall grass and weeds that effectively screened him from the closest of scrutinies. The headlights swept over him and the vehicle cruised past.

Bolan studied the house, seeking the best way to gain entry undetected. There were two windows fronting the strip of yard, plus the wooden door. Since diving through glass panes inevitably resulted in severe cuts to anyone foolish enough to attempt the feat—no matter how harmless they made it appear in the movies—he planned to go in through the door. He had to hit them hard and fast to prevent any of the terrorists from escaping.

The front door unexpectedly opened and out walked Orhan Mithat.

Wondering if he'd been spotted somehow, Bolan aligned the Uzi barrel between the bars and sighted on the stocky killer.

The terrorist moved to the edge of the porch and stretched. He gazed at the stars, then pulled a pack of cigarettes from a pocket.

Bolan held his fire. If he downed Mithat now, the rest might flee out the back. He wanted all three, wanted to put a permanent end to their bloody campaign of indiscriminate slaughter here and now.

The terrorist lighted his cigarette and gazed at the gloomy cemetery, then along the narrow road, not exhibiting a care in the world. He turned as someone else appeared.

Yeni Yurukoglu joined her leftist companion. They spoke in whispers with repeated glances at the doorway, as if plotting or afraid of being caught.

How easy it would be to down both, Bolan reflected. But the leader, Muzaffer Dora, was still unaccounted for.

Mithat and his companion conversed for a minute or so. When a car started climbing the hill from the south, Yeni quickly went inside. Mithat, however, stayed put, watching the vehicle's approach. He checked his watch once and nodded.

Something was going down, Bolan realized. He glanced to his right expectantly.

Soon a station wagon that had seen better days rattled onto the top of the hill and slowed. There were two shadowy forms in the front seat. The driver honked the horn, and Mithat waved and smiled.

Maybe it was Dora, Bolan speculated, then hugged the ground as the station wagon's beams flitted over his hiding place.

Mithat moved from the porch as the newcomers pulled off the road and parked to the left of the house. The driver killed the lights and out hopped two men, both bearded, both greeting the terrorist warmly. All three walked to the rear of the wagon and the newcomers took out a pair of apparently heavy suitcases, judging from the way they used both arms, and one of the men grunted when lifting his.

Bolan watched the trio enter the house and the door close. Whomever the new arrivals were, they rated a personal welcome from the terrorists. Did the Black Hand have members Arpinar hadn't known about? Unlikely. Could they be friends or relatives? Yes, but then why were the suitcases so heavy? The key to the riddle was there. Three items popped into the warrior's mind that would account for the weight—drugs, money or weapons. Since the intel indicated the band shied away from drugs, and since Pamir had been their money man and they hadn't had time to acquire a new source, the contents were likely to be weapons.

And people who supplied arms to terrorists were on the same level as their amoral customers. If they got caught in the cross fire, so be it.

The warrior had another thought. The band would be preoccupied with the bearded men for a while. No doubt at that moment greetings were being exchanged and no one was paying any attention to the door or the windows. Their mistake.

A look both ways confirmed no cars were approaching. Pushing erect, Bolan scaled the fence and leaped to the ground beyond. Speed was critical. He had to get to the house before they discovered him. In four long strides he crossed to the yard, unlimbering the Uzi on the run and raced straight for the front door.

The window shades remained undisturbed.

His feet flying, Bolan hit the porch and kept going, lowering his right shoulder and clamping his hands on the submachine gun. The terrorists were bound to hear his pounding footsteps; it couldn't be helped. But they would have a second at the most to react, not enough time to train a gun on the entrance. He hoped.

With a resounding, shattering crash the Executioner rammed into the wooden panel and snapped the lock. The inner jamb cracked and shattered, the door swinging inward. He went with it, trying to check his rush, finding himself in a living room, seeking targets right and left.

They were there, all right. Three of them, anyway, off to the left. The two arms dealers and Orhan Mithat were next to a couch on which the suitcases had been deposited. One of the cases had been opened, exposing an armory that would make any anarchist drool, and the taller of the newcomers held a Vz58 assault rifle, the well-designed copycat version of the Soviet AK-47, evidently in the act of giving it to Mithat.

Bolan fired while still in motion, swinging the Uzi toward the man with the Vz58, marking a line of red wet buttons across the man's chest.

Even as the warrior cut loose, the second arms dealer clawed for a weapon tucked under his loose-fitting beige shirt.

Mithat was already in high gear. Of the three hardmen, his reflexes were the best. At the instant the front door had buckled he'd whirled and darted for a doorway off the living room. He leaped after two paces and was in midair when crimson spray and bits of flesh erupted from the first dealer's back and spattered over the suitcases and the wall. By the time the second dealer produced a 9 mm Makarov pistol, he was out of sight.

Bolan's peripheral vision registered Mithat's departure. Part of him marveled at the man's quickness as he brought the Uzi several inches to the right and sent a swarm of Parabellum rounds into the second dealer's chest before the men could level the Makarov.

Then the big man moved, heading into a hallway with a kitchen at the far end, getting out of the living room before the terrorists could respond to his abrupt intrusion. There was no commotion at the front of the house, no cries of warning or panic from any of the rooms. Where were the other members of the Black

Hand? His eyes constantly scanning from front to back, he sped to the corner to find the kitchen empty. In the right-hand corner sat the gas stove, above it an open window.

The sight reminded Bolan of Izmir, of the clever tactic Mithat had used to escape. He ran to the window and looked to the north. Although he intensely disliked exposing his back to the hallway for even a second, he had to make certain.

Dangling from the next window over, the window to the room he'd entered, was Mithat. He stared at the slope fifteen feet below, gauging the distance. His head came up one final time and he spotted the Executioner.

Bolan saw Mithat's hands loosen from the sill, but he was ready, the Uzi angled properly, and all it took was slight pressure on the trigger to cause the SMG to sing its deadly song.

Perforated repeatedly in the act of falling, Orhan Mithat screamed and flapped his limbs, upending, caught up in a crash dive that terminated with the crunching thump of his cranium into the unyielding ground.

One down. Now to bag the other two. Spinning, the warrior straightened, thinking that he should replace the Uzi's magazine before he encountered another terrorist. Unfortunately an enemy had already encountered him.

Yeni Yurukoglu stood framed in the hallway, a pistol clutched in a two-handed grip, her stance wide and firm.

Staring the specter of Death in the face, Bolan acted on pure instinct. He tossed the Uzi to the right and went to the left, relying on the sailing submachine gun to distract her for a fraction of a second, a ploy no true professional would ever fall for. And as competent as Yeni Yurukoglu might be, she wasn't a pro, not in the same way as a seasoned hit man or a mercenary.

The woman took the bait, focusing on the Uzi instead of squeezing off shots. She recovered almost immediately, but "almost" meant the difference between life and eternity when confronted by a man as supremely skilled as the Executioner.

Bolan had the Desert Eagle drawn and aimed as he landed on his left side. She shifted and fired a hasty round that smacked into the kitchen floor inches from his chin. He answered with the roar of the hand cannon, the recoil bucking his arm upward.

Yeni took the big bore slug squarely in the chest. As if punted by an invisible giant, she hurtled backward onto the floor in a crumpled heap.

Not bothering to retrieve the Uzi, Bolan scrambled to the corner. He peeked out in time to see the woman's shoes disappearing around the opposite end. She'd manage to crawl to cover, leaving a wide red smear in her wake.

The warrior pushed into a crouch. He'd hurry after her if not for the missing wild card. Where the hell was Muzaffer Dora?

DORA GLANCED over his shoulder, ensuring no one was on his tail. He prided himself on the fact he never let his mental guard down, even for a minute. Stay alert and stay alive served as his personal motto.

There were pedestrians all around him, but none paid him the slightest attention. To them he was just another countryman, a Turk in black trousers, brown shirt and blue cap. The shirttail hung over his belt, concealing the M-63 machine pistol wedged at the small of his back.

He patted his left front pants pocket as he neared the garage that was his destination. A large sign in the front office window proclaimed the place closed, but dim lights were on within. Halting at the door he knocked three times, waited a second, then knocked twice more.

A burly form in grime-covered coveralls materialized, stared at Dora through the window for a moment, then went to admit him. "You're a half hour late. I was about to go home."

"It couldn't be helped," Dora replied. "I had to take the bus, and transferred twice as a safety precaution. The second time, the damn thing didn't show up at the stop on schedule."

"You don't have a car?"

"We do, but it wouldn't be wise to drive it around very much. The cops might have a description of it."

"I see." The man moved toward a doorway at the rear of the office. "Well, the job is done."

"As specified?" Dora asked, following.

They entered the garage proper, a huge triple-bay affair, one of which was empty. The second contained a car, its hood up and the carburetor off the engine.

Dora stopped and stared at the vehicle in the third bay, a brown minibus sporting a fresh coat of paint. Filling the transportation vacuum between full-size buses and ordinary taxicabs, the minibus was tremendously popular in the urban centers. They followed regular routes just likes buses, but carried more passengers than a traditional cab, nine to twelve at a time. And since the fares were cheaper than cabs, millions of Turks used the service daily.

"What do you think?" the mechanic inquired.

Moving over to the vehicle, Dora ran his hand over the cool metal hood and grinned. "You've done better than I dreamed possible. If I didn't know better, I would swear it is brand-new."

"Thank you. If you knew how many hours I have labored on this, you wouldn't be so amazed. I even put my regular customers on hold while I finished up."

"I knew I could count on you."

"Everything is exactly as you requested," the mechanic stated, stepping up to the grille. "The five hundred pounds of explosive are hidden in false compartments on the sides, between the door panels and in the fender wells. In effect this minibus is now a giant bomb."

"And the electronic detonator?"

"Climb in and see for yourself."

Dora got into the vehicle and studied the square black box attached to the underside of the dash. Two toggle switches were mounted on the front.

"Isn't that what you wanted?"

"Precisely."

"The toggle on the left will activate the system and turn on the detonator, but it won't go off until after the toggle on the right is pressed. That will begin the countdown sequence," the man explained.

"Ten seconds, as I asked?"

"Yes."

"Perfect."

The mechanic walked to the open door. "Have you told the others yet?"

"No. I plan to surprise them."

"Who will drive it?"

"I haven't decided yet."

The mechanic squared his shoulders. "Now, about the money you owe me."

Dora climbed down and reached into his left pocket to produce a wad of lira. "As I promised, Halova."

The man took the money and began to count the bills.

"Have I ever cheated you in the two years we've been doing business?" Dora asked, his right hand inching behind his back.

Halova kept on with his counting. "No. You know better. But I would be a shabby businessman if I didn't verify the full amount is here."

"And since this is the last time I will need your services, I would be a fool to let you live."

Startled, Halova looked up into the barrel of the machine pistol. He froze, then blurted the first thought that occurred to him. "Someone will hear the shot. You'll be caught."

"Who will think twice about a loud noise coming from a garage? Backfires are quite common, are they not?"

"Please don't," Halova begged. "I have a wife and three children."

"Not anymore," Dora declared, firing once, then stooping to retrieve the money.

A minute later, after dumping the body in the back seat of the car and opening the bay doors, Dora backed the minibus out and headed for the house where Orhan and Yeni should be concluding the latest purchases from the gun dealers. He turned on the radio and hummed along with the songs, pleased at the way everything was coming together.

He was still a mile from the hill when he spied the flashing lights at the top. Instead of continuing along the road and up to the summit, he turned off into a side street, parked the vehicle, got out and and walked to the corner. There had to be six or seven police cars, an ambulance and several other official vehicles parked near the house.

Something had gone terribly wrong.

Rage made Dora gnash his teeth. He knew he would never see his comrades again. Yeni wasn't much of a loss, but Orhan had been his best friend. His fists clenched, he hurried to the minibus and jumped into the driver's seat.

Now he was on his own. So be it. As long as he breathed, the Black Hand still existed. The authorities would probably believe they had put an end to the band. But they hadn't. They would learn the hard way—all Turkey would learn—that one determined man could make his mark in a spectacular fashion.

Such as the complete and utter destruction of the NATO summit, including the Türkiye Hilton and every last one of the NATO delegates.

22

Bolan had come full circle. He stared out a plate-glass window in the lobby of the plush Hilton and glimpsed his reflection. Here he was in Ankara again, dressed in a tailored dark blue suit, wearing a white shirt and tie, the Beretta resting under his left arm. An identification card and badge clipped to his jacket pocket informed all and sundry that he worked as a special agent for the justice ministry. The ID had been Sadria's idea. It enabled him to roam at will through the hotel.

Another limousine had just pulled up at the curb out front and disgorged its quota of NATO VIPs.

The warrior watched the officials move along the red carpet that had been laid out for the occasion. All morning delegates had been arriving. Now the clock on the wall indicated ten minutes until noon, and this latest batch should be the last. He noticed the security with satisfaction. The Turkish government had been exceedingly thorough.

Soldiers armed with submachine guns lined both sides of the curved drive connected to Tarhan Street. An honor guard of twenty troopers in their dress uniforms, all fully armed, stood on either side of the red carpet just outside the entrance. An additional contingent of twelve men stood at the ready on one side of the lobby. There were government agents and civilian police on every floor. Everyone who got off the elevator on the third floor, where the summit meetings were being held in the spacious conference chamber, had to pass through a metal detector and submit to having their briefcases searched.

The elaborate precautions were amply justified, as Bolan well knew. Muzaffer Dora wasn't the only terrorist who would give his eyeteeth for a crack at disrupting the summit. Any one of a score of radical groups would be glad to take the credit. But Dora was the warrior's special concern. He firmly believed the fanatic would make an attempt. How, he didn't know. When, he didn't know. But in his bones he felt the man would try.

"Has anyone ever told you that you are exceptionally good-looking?"

Bolan turned at the softly spoken words and smiled at the lovely woman who had shared her apartment, her food and her bed with him for the past few days. "Shouldn't you be concentrating on your work?"

"All stations have reported in and everything is fine," Sadria replied. She wore a prim gray dress for the occasion, the hem at midcalf, and a matching jacket that concealed her hardware. The newly arrived delegates walked through the glass doors, talking and joking, escorted by plainclothes police.

"I was wondering if you would like to join me for lunch?" Sadria asked. "There's a nice restaurant only three blocks from here."

"Leave?"

"Why not? You really must learn to relax more."

"I'll stay."

Sadria gestured at the soldiers outside. "What are you worried about? A terrorist couldn't get within fifty feet of the hotel without being shot to pieces. Besides, the summit will last for three days. You must eat sometime."

Every instinct told the warrior to stay there, but they had skipped breakfast that morning to arrive early at the hotel, and this might be the only chance for a meal in the next several hours.

"Come on," Sadria urged. "We do get an hour for lunch, don't we."

"All right."

They crossed the lobby, went down a hallway to the kitchen and exited the rear of the building. A pair of soldiers checked their IDs as they emerged.

"In a way I'm very glad we haven't been able to locate Dora yet," Sadria mentioned as they walked to her car.

"Why's that?"

"Because once we do, once he's out of the way, you'll be on your way back to America."

Bolan said nothing.

They climbed in, Sadria behind the wheel, and drove slowly to the side street bordering the Hilton to the north. She hung a left, taking them to Tarhan Street, then took a right when the traffic flow permitted.

"I'll be sorry to see you go," Sadria commented.

At the first block the light was red.

"Have you lost the power of speech?" Sadria asked, braking.

"No."

"Then you're trying to spare my feelings."

The light abruptly turned green and they pulled out.

"I told you I couldn't make any kind of a commitment," Bolan said, choosing his words with care.

"Yes," Sadria said quietly. "But I was hoping..." She let the sentence trail off.

An uncomfortable silence carried them through the next light and to the intersection where the restaurant was located. Sadria started to make a right into the parking lot when she glanced at the oncoming lane of vehicles and slammed on the brakes.

"Did you see that?"

"What?" Bolan responded.

"That brown minibus," Sadria said excitedly, executing a tight U-turn, causing cars behind her and those in the opposite lane to screech to a halt.

Twisting, Bolan saw the minibus in question driving at the speed limit. The driver's window was open and an elbow jutted out. From the outline of the head and shoulders visible through the rear window it appeared a man was at the wheel.

"I think Dora is driving," Sadria announced, putting the pedal to the metal.

The car leaped forward like a bloodhound on the scent of game, rapidly overtaking the minibus. Conveniently Dora stopped at a red light, and they pulled up behind the vehicle.

"We have to get a good look at the driver," Sadria said.

Bolan's mind raced. Why would Dora brazenly risk apprehension by driving past the summit site in broad daylight? The terrorist wasn't stupid; there had to be a reason why he'd put himself in jeopardy. But what? He glanced at the red light. "I'll take a look."

"Be careful," Sadria called after Bolan as he left the vehicle.

The warrior pushed the door shut as he moved forward, staying low so the driver of the minibus couldn't spot him in the rearview mirror.

A few passersby on the sidewalk stared at him quizzically.

Bolan rounded the front of the car and paused, knowing he had to move swiftly the moment he stepped into the open since the driver was bound to see him in the side mirror. He straightened and ran to the driver's door, his right hand under his jacket in case Sadria turned out to be correct.

She was.

Muzaffer Dora sat rigidly in the front seat, his eyes fixed on the avenue ahead, his fingers clamped tightly around the steering wheel. Beads of sweat caked his brow. His lips moved soundlessly, as if mouthing a silent prayer. He seemed oblivious to the world around him.

Whether guided by a sixth sense or having detected movement out of the corner of his left eye, Dora snapped his head around, caught sight of Bolan and stepped on the gas pedal. He betrayed no surprise at finding the big man beside his vehicle.

Bolan attempted to bring the Beretta to bear, his right hand sweeping out and around, but he was a hair too slow. He lunged as the minibus accelerated and succeeded in hooking his left forearm over the bottom of the window. In the back of his mind he entertained the notion of ramming the Beretta against Dora's temple and ordering the man to stop.

No such luck.

The Executioner was swept off his feet, his right arm banging against the door panel hard enough to make his elbow go numb. He hung on for his life, the minibus shooting through the intersection against the red light and rapidly reaching thirty miles an hour. On both sides brakes squealed in protest when oncoming drivers tried to avert catastrophe. He saw a car careering straight toward him and braced for the impact, expecting to be crushed to a mangled pulp. Instead the minibus roared ahead and the car missed it by inches.

Bolan fought to keep from falling. His body swayed, smacking repeatedly against the door, and his left arm started to slip. He couldn't keep his feet off the asphalt much longer, and he graphically envisioned what would happen should he lose his grip and plummet under the wheels of the minibus. He had a choice to make. Either hold on to the gun and inevitably fall, or cast the Beretta aside and use both hands to stay with the minibus. He opted for the latter. The Beretta clattered to the road and bounced away as Bolan gripped the window with his right hand and stared at his nemesis.

Dora still seemed out of it, ignoring the big man completely, his gaze riveted to the Hilton. Cars in the same lane blocked his path and he began weaving among them, mechanically swinging right and left.

The added motion compounded Bolan's predicament. He tried to pull himself up, to slide through the window, but the violent swerving kept throwing him off balance. Several times the toes of his shoes scraped on the asphalt, the friction threatening to tear him loose.

A horn blared behind the minibus as Sadria frantically tried to catch up.

Gritting his teeth, Bolan got his shoulders level with the window and began to squeeze inside. His gaze fell on a peculiar black box under the dashboard, on the other side of Dora, and a chilling insight goaded him to kick outward with all his might as he wiggled into the vehicle.

Dora calmly turned his head, sneered and lashed out with his left elbow.

Bolan took the blow on the mouth and felt his upper lip split. He couldn't bring his arms into play without losing his grip, so he continued to pull himself slowly in as the terrorist struck him three more times. Dazed, fireworks exploding before his eyes, Bolan lowered his head and managed to get his broad shoulders into the vehicle.

Dora went crazy, swinging his elbow again and again, cursing violently in Turkish, all the while spinning the wheel back and forth with his right hand as he passed cars in front of him.

The warrior's legs were whipped from side to side, throwing him off balance and preventing him from bracing himself long enough to fight back. At last the minibus straightened briefly and he looped his left arm around the terrorist's waist.

Dora bellowed in rage and flailed at the big man's head and back.

Wincing at the powerful punches, Bolan wished he could see how close they were to the Hilton. He guessed the minibus had to be less than a block away. As he struggled to raise his head and look, he saw Dora reach down and flick one of the toggle switches on the black box.

Bunching his shoulder and stomach muscles, Bolan gained enough leverage to slam his right fist into the terrorist's jaw. Dora was rocked sideways, but with a fanatical gleam in his eyes and the strength of a madman he returned the favor, giving as good as he got.

Bolan deliberately let his guard down long enough to glance through the windshield. He had to know where they were in relation to the hotel, to gauge how much time he had to dispose of his rabid foe. One look sufficed to show he was out of time. The minibus would reach the curved drive in seconds. Once Dora made the turn, the soldiers would pour a withering hail of lead into the vehicle. Even if the minibus did reach the Hilton, it would resemble a sieve when it got there. And so would the occupants.

As Dora reached for the second toggle, Bolan readily deduced the purpose and the outcome. All of his training and experience galvanized him into immediate action. Thrusting downward, he seized the terrorist's right arm, preventing Dora from touching the switch, while trying to seize control of the steering wheel with his other hand.

The terrorist resorted to a head butt, driving his forehead into the warrior's temple. For several costly ticks of the clock he let his right arm go slack, distracted from the toggle by his insane urge to smash this interloper who dared jeopardize his grand plan, to kill the man at all costs.

Bolan felt the terrorist's arm slacken and he promptly arched his back, elevated his chest and slashed a hand-sword strike into Dora's throat, his fingers as rigid as steel. The minibus veered sharply to the right as Dora released the wheel, his eyes wide in terror at having his larynx crushed. Blood spurted from the corners of his mouth as he grabbed at his neck.

Rocked against the rear window frame by the abrupt change of direction, Bolan looked out just as the minibus hit the curb and bounced a foot into the air. Agony flared in his abdomen when the vehicle came down with a brutal jolt. He saw a store looming in front of them, a market with a huge front window, and shoved off from the steering wheel. His chest and shoulders cleared the window, then he was tumbling end over end on hard concrete or asphalt.

The warrior felt himself slammed into something that jarred his very bones. Only dimly was he aware of lying on his stomach, of the taste of blood on his tongue and a ringing in his ears a heartbeat before an indescribable vacuum sucked his consciousness into an inky void.

BOLAN HEARD a jumble of voices and a song being sung in an unfamiliar language. It took several seconds for him to remember everything that had happened, and when he did his eyes snapped open and he automatically tried to sit up.

"Whoa, Striker. Not so fast."

The sight of Hal Brognola standing on his right momentarily confused Bolan. "Hal?"

"In the flesh. How do you feel?"

"Like death warmed over," the Executioner answered honestly, and suddenly realized he was lying in a bed and wearing a green hospital gown.

"Well, you should. You tried to dent a wall with your head. You've been out over fourteen hours."

Bolan reached up and gingerly touched his sore scalp. "I don't feel any stitches."

"You won't," Brognola said. "Your head is in one piece, although I understand you did chip the wall."

"Funny."

"The doctor says you suffered a concussion, but in a week or so you'll be almost as good as new."

Glancing around, Bolan recognized the trappings of a typical hospital room. "Am I still in Ankara?"

"Sure are. I was en route to Germany to check on a situation going bad when Matthews in communications relayed a message from the new director of the Turkish justice ministry's Terrorism Department," the big Fed explained. "It wasn't much of a detour to fly here and check on you."

"Thanks," Bolan said sincerely.

"The President is quite pleased with your performance. Had Dora reached the Hilton, it's doubtful there would be anything left of it. I understand his minibus contained enough explosives to destroy half a city block.''

''Dora is dead, I take it?''

Brognola nodded. ''The director told me he crashed into a store and rammed into a row of cash registers. He was thrown through the windshield and the glass made mincemeat out of his face and neck.''

''Too bad.''

''The Black Hand is history. The Turkish president wanted to bestow a medal on you, but I convinced him that you're the shy, retiring type.''

''I don't know what I'd do without you.''

''Probably live longer,'' Brognola said, only partly in jest. He walked to the window and stared out at Ankara's skyline. ''I know you're not the type to lie around even under a doctor's orders, but a week of R and R wouldn't hurt.''

''You want me to stay here? What about Germany?''

''It'll wait. Hasn't reached the intervention stage yet.''

Smiling, the big Fed moved to the foot of the bed. ''Don't be so eager to get back in the saddle. The new director led me to believe the two of you had some business to finish.''

Bolan sat up. ''So who is this new director?''

''Now I know you're not goldbricking or you would have guessed by now,'' Brognola quipped, nodding at the doorway.

In walked Sadria Inonu, looking stunning in a stylish green dress and high heels, grinning. ''Apparently

I misjudged our president. He pushed for my nomination and it was accepted."

"Congratulations."

"Not only that," Sadria went on, "but he graciously gave me a week off as a bonus for concluding the Black Hand affair so nicely."

Brognola stepped toward the door. "I'd better go fetch the doc. He wanted to check you after you awakened." He gave a little wave and was gone.

"I like him," Sadria stated. "He's a very nice man."

"You don't know him as well as I do," Bolan grumbled.

Bending, Sadria drew a finger seductively down the warrior's chest. "It's not him I want to know."

Bolan knew there were worse fates than spending a week with a beautiful, passionate woman, and his battle-weary soul could use a little R and R. A brief respite from the hellgrounds, then back to War Everlasting. It was a soldier's life.

The hunters become the hunted as Omega Force clashes
with a former Iraqi military officer in the next episode of

by PATRICK F. ROGERS

In Book 3: TARGET ZONE, Omega Force blazes a trail deep
into the heart of Sudan. Trapped and surrounded by hostile forces, they must break out at any cost to launch a
search-locate-annihilate mission.

With capabilities unmatched by any other paramilitary
organization in the world, Omega Force is a special ready-
reaction antiterrorist strike force composed of the best
commandos and equipment the military has to offer.

Take
4 explosive books
plus a
mystery bonus
FREE

Mail to: Gold Eagle Reader Service

Mail to: Gold Eagle Reader Service
3010 Walden Ave.,
P.O. Box 1394
Buffalo, NY 14240-1394

YEAH! Rush me 4 FREE Gold Eagle novels and my FREE mystery gift. Then send me
4 brand-new novels every other month as they come off the presses. Bill me at the low
price of just $13.80* for each shipment—a saving of over 10% off the cover prices for all
four books! There is NO extra charge for postage and handling! There is no minimum
number of books I must buy. I can always cancel at any time simply by returning a
shipment at your cost or by returning any shipping statement marked "cancel." Even if I
never buy another book from Gold Eagle, the 4 free books and surprise gift are mine to
keep forever.   164 BPM AEQ6

_____

Name   (PLEASE PRINT)

_____

Address   Apt. No.

_____

City   State   Zip

_____

Signature (if under 18, parent or guardian must sign)

*Terms and prices subject to change without notice. Sales tax applicable in NY. This offer
is limited to one order per household and not valid to present subscribers. Offer not
available in Canada.

© 1991 GOLD EAGLE   AC-92R

In the battlefield of covert warfare America's toughest
agents play with lethal precision in the third installment of

SLAM

by DAN MATTHEWS

In Book 3: SHADOW WARRIORS, hostile Middle East leaders
are using the drug pipeline to raise cash for a devastating nu-
clear arsenal and the SLAM commando unit is ordered to dis-
mantle the pipeline, piece by piece.

In the aftermath of a
brutal apocalypse,
a perilous quest for survival.

EARTH BLOOD

by **JAMES AXLER**

The popular author of DEATHLANDS® brings you an action-
packed new postapocalyptic survival series. Earth is laid to
waste by a devastating blight that destroys the world's food
supply. Returning from a deep-space mission, the crew of the
Aquila crash-land in the Nevada desert to find that the world
they knew no longer exists. Now they must set out on an
odyssey to find surviving family members and the key to
future survival.

In this ravaged new world, no one knows who is friend or
foe . . . and their quest will test the limits of endurance and
the will to live.

Available in November at your favorite retail outlet.

GOLD
EAGLE ®

EB1

Don't miss out on the action in these titles featuring
THE EXECUTIONER, ABLE TEAM and PHOENIX FORCE!